Suburban Pornography

Acknowledgments

Thank you Brian Kaufman and Anvil Press; literary brothers and sisters Jason Copple, T. Anders Carson, Mark McCawley, Harold Hoefle, Bill Brown, Kenneth J. Harvey, Salvatore Difalco, Len Gasparini, Dan Fante, Laura Hird, Philip David Alexander, Michael Bryson, David Rose, Frances Ward, Vern Smith, and Max Maccari; old and new friends here and there; family; and, above all, Andrea, Samuel and Willem.

Earlier versions of some of these stories have appeared in *Exact Fare Only 2*, *blood and aphorisms*, *Hammered Out*, *Liticaphobia*, and *Let Slip the Vermin of Peace*.

Suburban Pornography
and Other Stories

Matthew Firth

[signed] Matt Firth
Halifax / October 2006

ANVIL PRESS | VANCOUVER

Suburban Pornography
Copyright © 2006 by Matthew Firth

All rights reserved. No part of this book may be reproduced by any means without the prior written permission of the publisher, with the exception of brief passages in reviews. Any request for photocopying or other reprographic copying of any part of this book must be directed in writing to ACCESS: The Canadian Copyright Licensing Agency, One Yonge Street, Suite 800, Toronto, Ontario, Canada, M5E 1E5.

LIBRARY AND ARCHIVES CANADA CATALOGUING IN PUBLICATION

Firth, Matthew, 1965—

　　Suburban pornography / Matthew Firth.

ISBN: 1-895636-77-9

　　I. Title.

PS8561.I66S92 2006　　　　C813'.54　　　C2006-905158-5

Printed and bound in Canada
Cover design: Typesmith Design
Interior design & typesetting: HeimatHouse

Represented in Canada by the Literary Press Group
Distributed by the University of Toronto Press

The publisher gratefully acknowledges the financial assistance of the Canada Council for the Arts, the Book Publishing Industry Development Program (BPIDP), and the Province of British Columbia through the B.C. Arts Council and the Book Publishing Tax Credit.

Anvil Press Inc.
P.O. Box 3008, Main Post Office
Vancouver, B.C. V6B 3X5 CANADA
www.anvilpress.com

For Andrea — who else?

Contents:

Sheila Crawford Sucks Cocks   9
August, 1974   19
Missed Bus   29
Job Action   39
The Summer of No Love   57
Giants   77
Begotten, Not Made   85
The Centre   91
One Night in Oktober   107
Everybody Loses   115
Smooth with the Ladies   121
Aquamarine   137
Suburban Pornography   149
Bruised Ribs   157
The Last Time   165
On a Quiet Residential Street   169
A Serious Deterrent   177

Sheila Crawford Sucks Cocks

On the sidewalk in front of my house Clarence tells me, "Sheila Crawford sucks cocks. She does. I seen it."

"Like fuck you have. Where?"

"Up the alley. In Rachel Stevens' old man's car. I seen her there a couple times. She sucks cocks. I'm tellin' yah she does. Cross my heart."

"Like fuck. She's in Grade 6."

"Yeah, maybe, but she's failed at least twice. You seen the tits on her?"

"Yeah. Still, she's younger than us. She's gotta be. She's maybe twelve. No more than that."

"No, no. Same as us. Thirteen."

"Yeah?"

"Yeah. And not too young to suck cocks, I'm telling yah."

"So you said."

"Seen it with my own eyes."

"Who then? Tell me whose cocks she sucks."

"Not yours."

"Fuck off and tell me."

"Kevin Forbes and Terry Watson, just the other day."

"Both of them?"

"Yup. First Kevin, then Terry. One waited while the other one got blowed. Then the other hopped in the car and he got blowed. I seen it. It took about five minutes."

"Fuck off."

"I seen it. I'm tellin' yah."

"They're in high school. Grade 11 or something. My brother's age."

"Yeah. That's just it. Sheila don't wanna suck our cocks. She wants to suck high school guys' cocks. Get it?"

"Get what? They're fuckn using her. Fuckn slut."

"Yeah, maybe, but she's using them too."

"Yeah, how?"

"Don't know that yet. Just know Sheila and Rachel wanna hang out with high schoolers."

"Fuck sakes."

"Yeah."

Clarence takes me up the alley to show me where.

There's Rachel Stevens' old man's car just like he said. I look at the car and try to picture the blowjobs Clarence described outside my house.

In a way, it doesn't surprise me. A lot of shit happens in the alley. My brother's told me some of it. Some of it I've seen myself. And there's also what me and Clarence have found messing around. One time we were catching grasshoppers, putting them in jars with holes punched in the lids. Later we fried the grasshoppers with magnifying glasses. It's juvenile shit but we can't seem to give it up.

In the uncut grass behind some of the garages where we caught the bugs we found empty model glue packets, used condoms and busted beers bottles. We found old skin mags another time. Someone had beat off on some of the pages and then chucked the magazines. Me and Clarence thought we'd struck gold anyway. We ripped out the pages that weren't spunked on and divided them in half. Clarence liked the big tits. I liked the women with dark hair. Clarence said fuck the dark hair. Who cares what their hair looks like. You can see that walking down the street. It's the tits and cunts that matter. I looked at him and nodded. I was embarrassed not knowing as much as him. I took my pictures home and stared at the tits and cunts, trying to ignore the hair. I beat off rubbing my cock against the mattress of my bed. I knew I was supposed to stick my cock in their cunts or have them suck my cock. I didn't know how that would feel. I didn't know how they would do it. I wasn't going to ask Clarence. I was embarrassed enough.

Later, after dinner, me and Clarence sneak up the alley. It's just getting dark. He says some of the high schoolers were hanging out down the block at Sheila's place after school.

"She'll suck their cocks, you'll see."

"They'll see us."

"No fuckn way. We climb on top of the Vincelli's garage. They won't see fuck all. They all got their eyes closed anyways. And it's almost dark."

"How we gonna see anything?"

"You'll see, believe me. You'll fuckn make yourself see."

Me and Clarence are on the roof of the Vincelli's garage. Three older boys wait around. Rachel Stevens comes out from her yard with Sheila and opens her old man's car. The old man never seems to drive it. I don't think he works any more. He's older, probably twenty years older than Rachel's mom. I've seen Rachel's mom at the bus stop. She's not bad for someone's mom. She smokes long cigarettes waiting for the bus. She wears dark red lipstick. She always looks at me but doesn't say hello. She knows who I am but won't speak to me. It scares me a little. She has beautiful, dark hair.

Sheila and Rachel stand around talking to the boys. The boys start fidgeting and looking about nervously. One guy keeps looking back down the alley at my street. I don't recognize them. They don't live around here. My brother probably knows them from high school.

They do rock paper scissors and then one guy gets in the car with Sheila. She blows him in the back seat, just like Clarence said. Then the other guy. I can't believe it.

"Is she gonna suck off all three of them?"

"Just watch. How the fuck do I know? This is fuckn too much. What if her brothers showed up right now?"

I look at Clarence. I'd forgotten about Sheila's four older brothers.

The third guy goes over to the car. But then Sheila gets out and Rachel gets in. Sheila stands there, leaning on the car, playing with her hair. The two guys she blowed stand like fuckn apes, unable to speak. Meanwhile, Rachel's not blowing the other guy. She's fucking him. Or he's fucking her. She's stretched out on the back seat of the car. The car door is open. The guy's half in half out of the car. I can see his skinny white ass in the half dark. The other two guys look like they can't fucking believe it. One of them starts playing with Sheila's tits. Then the other guy starts rubbing her crotch but Sheila backs away from that. She starts rubbing their crotches instead. The one guy takes his cock out. He's got a hard-on again. But Sheila doesn't blow him. She beats him off. The guy comes a second time, looking over Sheila's shoulder at his friend fucking Rachel. The other guy must be squirrelly or something because he can't come. He pulls away from Sheila right when the guy in the car finishes off with Rachel. Rachel pulls the condom off the guy and chucks it into the tall grass by the Vincelli's garage. The squirrelly guy takes off up the alley. He's lost his nerve.

I can't fucking believe it. I've got a hard-on pressed against the roof of the Vincelli's garage. Clarence has a look on his face like he's a thousand miles away.

"What now?"

"Fuckn shut up and watch before they hear."

But they don't hear. And they're done, anyway. Sheila and Rachel go into Rachel's backyard, giggling and waving to the two remaining high school boys. They stand and watch and then fuck off down the alley, back to my street.

"Clarence, what now?"

"Will you shut up and fuck off."

Now Clarence is sort of over on his side with his back to me. I can tell by the way his voice is strained that he's beating off. I climb down from the garage and go home. I go straight up to the bedroom I share with my brother. He isn't around. He must be out somewhere. Maybe he gets his cock sucked by Sheila Crawford.

I take my skin mag pictures out from my dresser and look at them and think about Sheila. I look at the mouths of the women in the pictures. I take off my pants and underwear and lie down on the bed. Then I look down at my cock mashed against the mattress. I put the pictures next to my cock, trying to imagine the women sucking me off. My cock looks huge next to their mouths. I think for a second that I'm a giant, a great big hairy beast with a cock a city block long. The women in the pictures are tiny as sparrows by comparison. They fly around and then land on the end of my cock. They sing a weird little birdsong. The women look up at me past my giant cock with their jet-black sparrow eyes. Then they try to suck my enormous cock with their tiny mouths. But they're not birds. They're women with puckered pink mouths. I move the pictures around a bit and rub my cock against the crinkled pages. I come, then shove the pictures away.

When I go back up the alley the next day after school I see it. It says *SHEILA CRAWFORD SUCKS COCKS* on the side of the Vincelli's garage in red spray paint. Clarence must have done it. Rachel Stevens' old man's car is where it always is. I just kind of nose around, loiter a bit. I look over at the car and start rubbing my cock through the pocket of my pants. Then I hear the gate to Rachel's yard open and Rachel and Sheila come out.

"What the fuck are you doing standing around here Matthew?"

Sheila says it like she's ten years older than me instead of the same age. I can't answer her. I look at Rachel and think about how she let that high school boy fuck her. She smiles at me. It's a condescending smile. Then she points at the Vincelli's garage.

"Fuck Sheil, see that?"

"Yeah, so what. Matthew probably fuckn wrote it. Right after he beat off on top of the garage last night."

I'm getting nervous. "Wasn't me."

"Wasn't you who wrote it or wasn't you who beat off?"

I don't know how to answer. Sheila and Rachel look at me. I feel like I'm shrinking right before their eyes. I'm not a giant, more like a sparrow. They're in Grade 6. I'm in Grade 8. I shouldn't be this fucked up around them but I can't help it. Where's Clarence when you need him? But I came up here without him on purpose. I wanted to spy on Sheila and Rachel again without him. I didn't know he wrote that shit on the garage. If Sheila's brothers see it they'll kick the shit out of Clarence or anybody they think did it, including me.

It looks like Sheila and Rachel don't give a fuck about the graffiti. They just stand there waiting for me to say something. I'm here so I may as well say something. I came up the alley for a reason. All I come up with is, "What about me?" I can't say, "Will you suck my cock, Sheila?" I can't bring myself to say that. But I also don't want to take off down the alley like a pussy, like that guy last night who lost his nerve.

I say it again, "What about me?" It sounds desperate, pathetic, like I'm five years old asking for candy or a toy.

There's a short silence and then Sheila sort of starts holding her breath. Her cheeks puff out and turn red.

Rachel shakes her head. She's got really nice dark hair like her mom.

Then Sheila bursts out laughing.

Rachel's all business. She stops shaking her head for a second and says, "You just don't get it, do you?"

I don't know what to say. What don't I get? I have no idea. That's exactly my problem.

Sheila stops laughing and Rachel glares at me one more time. They both walk away down the alley, back to my street.

I look over at the garage. *SHEILA CRAWFORD SUCKS COCKS*. It says so right there in enormous letters on the side of the Vincelli's garage. But she won't suck mine.

» » »

August, 1974

"I'm gonna get his room now. I'm gonna get George's fuckn room."

She struts around the park calling it out, cigarette in one hand. A leather-beaded purse hangs off her shoulder, swivelling round as she walks. She gestures. Points the smoke at someone she knows. High as a kite. She looks like Susan Dey as Laurie Partridge—long brown straight hair, flat on top of her head, parted perfectly in the centre. Brown eyes. But eyes fiercer than Susan Dey. Jeans tight at her hips. Tan clogs. Checked shirt knotted over her belly. Glimmer of white flesh. A slutty version of Laurie Partridge.

"I'm gonna get his room now. I'm gonna get George's fuckn room. I'm done sharing a room with my brat sister. Gonna get George's room now. What's left of it."

Guy to my left stands among six or seven teenagers. Long black hair. Platform shoes. Tight T-shirt—Keep on Truckin'. Calls out to her, "That mean we can screw inside now? Instead ah here in the park?" He grabs his crotch. Tongue lolls out. Laughter all around him.

She's unbothered. Euphoric. Not embarrassed that her business is public.

Calls back, "You got that right, Brian. You got that fuckn right. You tell all your twat friends too. 'Cause I'm gonna get his room now. I'm gonna get that little fucker's room."

She points her smoke at the sky. Arm rigid. Victory salute.

» » »

Sirens. Sirens brought us. A distant whirring got stronger and stronger. Cops? Ambulance? Someone said they saw smoke. They were over on Dundurn coming back from Mac's Milk, saw smoke way down the street, past the Brewers Retail even.

All the boys assembled. Roger Wills chaired.

"There's a fire. Way down Dundurn. As far as Main. Somebody's place burnin' up. Let's go. Together."

My older brother was there. I looked up at him. He glanced back at our house. "Get on your bike."

I was the only one who rode, only way to keep up with the older boys.

» » »

Houses smaller down here, past Melbourne Avenue. Hill Street. Over the railway bridge. To where Canada Street butts up against Dundurn. I'd never gone as far on my bike before, at least not in this direction. Not north. A different world, north. Kids swear and holler in the streets. Kids run around with no shoes. Dirty hands, dirty faces. No one cares. No one gets blasted for looking grubby, for swearing. Kids younger than me crossing Dundurn on their own. Shouting at cars to fuck off. Fuck this. Fuckn faggot that. Shitlicker. One I'd never heard before.

I'm cautious. Scared, but don't want my brother to know. Cross over the railway bridge with him, Roger, John Marcetelli, Dominic Delello, Ed and Walter Zshavski, Johnny White, various Coogans.

I look down from the railway bridge. Oily tracks. Ties leech creosote. Paper Dominion grocery bags wet and frayed, coming apart. Pitched bottles smashed. Rusty nails, broken glass. Overturned grocery store cart. Dilapidated beer cases.

A guy lies back drinking. Looks up at me. Right at the instant I spot him. Not that old, really—probably forty. But to me he looks ancient, an old man. Dirty hair. Grubby clothes. Creased, brown skin. Yellow eyes. And pissed off. He looks absolutely pissed off at everything, including me—especially me. Like I'm everything he hates. Like if he could, he'd reach up from under the bridge, grab my skinny ankles, pull me off my bike and drag me down into his stink—teach me a lesson, keep me there till I stunk too. He holds my gaze till I look away.

>> >> >>

The stink of alcohol, cigarettes, body odour. Blinds drawn. Halo of sunlight against nicotine-yellowed material. Light trying to penetrate. Glint of orange. Darkness puts up a fight.

"Where you hidin'? Come on out, Georgie boy."

"Momma?"

All the time he says it. All the time she hears it. All the time she ignores it.

"Momma?"

"Quit yer blubberin'. You got it comin'. Little fucker."

Girls out of the house. Out slutting around somewheres. Just momma, daddy, and George at home.

"Get those bitches outa my sight." First thing he said when he stepped through the door.

Feet shuffle heavy on the green painted hardwood. Wallpaper stained, peeling away. Mirror cracked. Tiger-Cats pennant hangs limp off the mirror frame, a remnant of the '72 Cup. Some junk looted from school piled on the dresser—school supplies, shit ripped off other kids. Stuff to sell for smokes. Stuff to burn that will not sell.

"Momma?"

"Don't put up a fuss now, Georgie boy."

Daddy stops, exhales a plume of alcohol. Listens.

"Momma?"

Was straight to the tavern after work at three. Beer and whisky. Payday. Round after round. Liquid supper. Home pissed on the Barton bus, then Main West, scuttled out at Dundurn. Seven o'clock back to the squat house on Canada Street.

Only so many places George can hide in a room seven feet by eight. Small, single bed, mattress drooping, up against one wall. A few lonely shirts, trousers hang in the closet. Old chair, dirty underwear and socks on the floor. Couple *Mad* magazines. Hockey cards. Empty cigarette packs—Export A. Same brand as daddy, same brand as momma, same brand as his two sisters. Packs of matches. Lots of packs of matches. Stolen from Becker's.

George plays with matches. Lights things on fire in the park. In the small backyard—twenty feet wide by maybe fifteen deep, broken chain-link fence at the back slopes down to the railway tracks. George burns newspapers. Dominion bags. School books. Old cigarette packs. Rags. Rags soaked in oil. Throws them down on the tracks. Burns piles of leaves. Any junk by the tracks. Any junk he can get his hands on that'll burn. Wants to set a train on fire. George dreams of burning trains. Trains that jump the tracks, fly through the air, plough into his house and destroy it in a blazing fireball—his entire family incinerated in seconds.

"Georgie, it's Thursday. Payday. Come and get some."

Daddy always waits till a train goes by. Then he'll pounce. The roar of the diesel drowns out his son's cries. Fuckn trains never pass when you need them, he thinks.

"Momma?"

Room swims and spins round daddy. Bit of filtered sunlight blinds him when he turns. Thinks he heard something from the closet. Daddy feels nauseous. Smells sulphur. *Scritch scritch* of matches striking. Maybe Georgie lighting up a fag? A burst of flame. A muffled, "What? Fuck?!" Then down goes daddy, felled, right into the drooped mattress. Piss drunk. Passed out. Burnt out. Ker-plunk. Before the train. Before he could pounce.

Oily rags stuffed into the mattress. Sunlight trickling through. *Scritch scritch* go the matches. Bits of orange sunlight. More light. Yellow licks of flame.

Momma comes up the tattered stairs. No tears. Eyes all dried up. She cries for no one. Tears beat out of her a long time ago. She grabs the doorknob; holds it closed. Ignores George's pounding. Ignores the smoke coming out from under the door. Ignores George's wailing, failing voice like she's done so many times before. Thinks only of breaking the circle.

She reeks of alcohol, cigarettes, and body odour. Now, too, of smoke—white-knuckled grasp on the doorknob.

Blood of her family invisible on her hands. She pries off her wedding band. Tosses it. Hopes it melts in the fire. Last gasp from George, then she darts for the street.

>> >> >>

I dream of trains. There's a switching yard a few blocks from my house, over by the Westinghouse plant. All through the night trains crash, coupling together. In my dreams the trains are like in a children's book—smiling faces on the front of the engine, toys and treats for good little boys and girls on the other side of the mountain. I dream about smiling, friendly trains, peppermint drops as big as basketballs, lollypops as big as trees. Idiot grinning clowns like friendly giants. Where I live, nothing burns. No one dreams of burning trains, of incinerated families or the joy of scorched brothers.

>> >> >>

I know George. He was in my Grade 4 class last year. Seems ages ago now. Summer of slow burn.

>> >> >>

Papers come out with details. Papers I don't read. Everyone gets *The Spec* on the block. Story trickles down.

Details spilled, passed along, up the block. Roger told John, who told my brother. I was there. By the curb. Hands in pockets.

"Father diddled him."

I look around. Their voices hushed. A word I don't know.

"Father smoked. They all smoked. George. Both sisters. The mother. The father."

George? He was the same age as me.

"George burned the bed. He couldn't get out. Torched himself too. The father was a drunk."

A word I know.

"Passed out on the bed. Burned his old man. Killed him. Old man diddled him night after night."

That word again.

Eyebrows up. Heads nod. Hands in pockets. They know.

» » »

"I'm gonna get his room now. I'm gonna get George's fuckn room."

She's still calling it for all to hear. Fire trucks have come and gone. Ambulance gone. Police hang around. Cops'll want to talk to her at some point.

"I'm gonna get his room now. I'm gonna get George's fuckn room."

The guys by the butt end of the street look over at her. One says, "Old man's gone. We can all go over and fuck that slut. You know, take turns. Like the old man probably done with his buddies and that kid." More laughter.

I look at my brother, confused.

"On your bike. Excitement's over."

I grab my two-wheeler. Peddle away like mad. School starts in a week. No George this year. In my class or any other. I'm nine years old. Ten in October.

» » »

Missed Bus

I call the Hamilton Street Railway's Bus Check number for my stop. The Stephen Hawking-esque voice says, "Bus Check Schedule. Route 7. Locke. Next bus to King Street and John Street in four minutes. Following bus in twenty-four minutes."

That automated voice never lies. It's saved me from freezing for twenty minutes at a time on many occasions, staring up Dundurn Street. A beautiful invention: Bus Check. Way better than the old days with those hard-to-decipher paper schedules, with all their different departures depending on whether it was rush hour, a weekend, a holiday, a bloody full moon, or some such thing. I could never make sense of those schedules. But the blue-rinse grannies always could, cheekily puttering around the corner with their walkers just as the bus pulled into the stop. Bus Check just tells you what you need to know: when the next bus will arrive at *your* stop.

So I sprint out the door at exactly twenty-three minutes to midnight, thirty seconds after hanging up the phone. I live right around the corner from the stop on Dundurn Street. I know four minutes means bolt it, now!

The closest call I've had and still made it was "Next bus in two minutes." I had a "Next bus in one minute," once. I nearly dropped dead to the floor. I ran—untied shoelaces fluttering in the cold breeze—to the stop, only to catch a whiff of diesel as Route 7 pulled away. Had my shoes been tied, I might have beat it to the next stop and boarded, but the god of public transit was conspiring against me that night.

There is nothing worse than missing a bus. I tell my girlfriend this time and time again. She just doesn't understand my urgency, my panic—she being of some sort of suave, laidback, Eastern European, the-bus-will-get-here-when-it-gets-here mentality. She's yet to call Bus Check, probably has no idea the service exists.

Me, I'm white-knuckled when it comes to catching the bus. I like precision. Especially when getting to work on time hangs in the balance. And that's another thing. I hate getting to work early. Not even two, three minutes. That's *my* time, not theirs. I'm not selling my labour to the boss for free. Fuck the white hats. That's always been my philosophy.

So if I time the bus just right, I can step through the doors at the Wesley Centre at exactly midnight to start my shift. Of course, that's after pushing through the crowd of thugs waiting for the night-programme to begin: the huddled masses eager for a bowl of reheated, leftover soup ("These fucking noodles are too soggy," someone always complains) and a hard bench or a hard floor to sleep on; one more night out of the cold. It's been a nasty winter so far: two dead from exposure on the city streets already.

I digress. Back to the bus. I'm safely around the corner now, semi-race-walking to the stop. But I don't hear the bus's groan as it pulls away from its perch at the top of Dundurn Street, two hundred metres or so away. That's the end of the line, where Dundurn stops at the foot of the Niagara escarpment. "The mountain" to locals. The Locke bus always makes a wide, 180-degree turn on the steep hill. The driver then sits and drinks coffee from a Thermos, maybe reads the paper till it's time to start the run back downtown. My stop is the second on the route. You can usually see the bus sitting at the top of the street, in among the trees on the side of the mountain.

So I look over my shoulder as I walk and check up the street. No bus coming. I can't even see it. It must be up there. It's supposed to be at my stop in a minute or so.

I get to the stop. My pulse quickens. Look up the street. No bus. Check my pocket for my bus pass for the two-thousandth time in my life. Check the Bus Check phone number pasted to the pole, just to be certain. Look up the street. No bus. Check my watch. It's at least four minutes since I hung up the phone. What gives?

Check up the street again. No bus. Check my toque. Pull my gloves up tightly onto the cuffs of my coat. Check up the street. No bus. Check that my wallet and keys are in my pockets. Check my bus pass again. Take one glove off and check that my nuts are still hanging at my crotch. Then check up the street. Still no bus.

I look at my watch again. Six minutes since Stephen Hawking told me the bus was coming in four minutes. Fuck sakes. I'll be late for work. Once downtown, I'll have to run from Gore Park over to the Wesley Centre to make it on time. I fidget. Kick clumps of snow on the pavement. Peer into the empty newspaper box. Being a midnight commuter there are no papers left. Look up Dundurn again. No bus in sight.

Eight minutes since Stephen Hawking. This is serious. I'll be late for sure and my supervisor will kick my ass. The clients at the centre will complain if they have to wait an extra three minutes for me to serve their soup and stale sandwiches. They'll be on my case all night, probably not relenting till after I serve breakfast.

It's a shit job, anyway: soup kitchen cook. Mostly I get fed nothing but grief; the clients taking out the day's frustrations on me, like anyone would, like spouses bitching at spouses at the end of the workday commute. But some of the clients are okay. And most are fast asleep by two o'clock. Once I clean up the soup and sandwiches, do the dishes, I usually get two, three hours to myself to read a book, write a letter or two, maybe play chess with Harold, the guy who cleans the washrooms at the Centre. Of course, that usually means putting up with Harold's attempts to convert me. He's a devout Jehovah's Witness. After Friday night shifts, I've seen him change out of his custodian's greens into a three-piece suit to hit the streets and save some souls.

Shit, that's ten minutes now! Something's up with this bus. I've got two choices. Cab it, which I've done in a pinch. But it's about fourteen bucks to get to the Centre by cab. Payday's a full ten days off, so that's not the most favoured option. The other choice is to investigate. Maybe the driver nodded off. Maybe his watch is broken. Maybe he has no clue what Stephen Hawking told me ten minutes ago. Maybe he still goes by the old paper schedule. Or the dude just doesn't care if I'm late for work. He likely hates the late-night shift anyway, having to deal with weirdoes, drunks, and whores all night. In some sense, I can't blame him for not wanting to start his run. We're both in the same line of work: providing essential public services to those in need.

Okay, that's eleven minutes. I can't stand here another second. But it's still a tough choice. If I leave now to run up to the top of Dundurn, the bus might suddenly lurch out from the trees. Then I'll be stranded between stops, like a mouse scrambling for cover as a hawk swoops down for the kill. I'll be screwed. I'll miss the bus and that'll be that. But I can't wait here and do nothing. The anxiety is killing me.

I sprint up the street, covering the two hundred metres in fifty seconds, which isn't bad for a nearly middle-aged slug in winter boots.

The bus *is* here. Only it's tucked back in the trees more than usual. The lights are on. The engine is silent. The driver's seat is empty.

I stomp over. Knock on the door. Nothing. I look up through the windows. Nothing to see from this angle but the chiropractor and gum adverts above the seats. I knock again. Nothing. Is the guy off having a shit in the woods? Maybe.

Then I hear something from inside the coach. Noises. Movements. I gotta find out what the hell is going on here. Maybe the driver's getting worked over by thugs. I jam a gloved hand between the panes of glass on the divided door, prying them apart. I wedge myself through and emerge on the other side. Step up the two steps and hear more movements. Look to my left. There's the driver, the bastard. He's taking his break all right. Taking it way too far. The dude's screwing some broad, getting a little midnight action while I get worked up down the street waiting for this bus to take me to work. And he's banging her right on the bus, in the first seat, the one right behind the driver that's reserved for the infirm. The one the blue-rinse grannies always grab. I always see them sitting there, leaning forward, watching every move the driver makes, anxious they'll miss their stop. They ring that bell the exact second the driver leaves the stop before theirs. They covet those bus seats like most normal folks covet front row seats at a Leafs or Habs game.

The driver doesn't flinch when I come on board the bus. He's still mostly dressed, his tan polyester trousers down around his shins; his bus driver's brown cardigan sweater dishevelled. Greasy hair messed. Dandruff on his shoulders. His white ass up in the air. He's supporting himself with one hand planted on the floor of the bus. The other is scrunched under the woman. His ass drives like a drill. He must be almost finished. Must know he's late for his run and wants to wrap this up.

The woman I can barely see. She's wearing fuck-me boots. The rest of her is hard to make out; she's mostly swaddled in her winter greatcoat, a kind of pukey, pea-green number. I see a tangle of peroxide-blonde hair and one grubby hand. Maybe she's working too. Maybe she's providing an essential service as well.

And then I glance up. There's a cane resting against the seat behind the one they're screwing on. Well, fuck sakes. What do you call this then, I wonder? At least they're entitled to be in that seat. An older girl, she is.

I drag my feet. Clear my throat. Still nothing. She's likely half-asleep. I see a glimmer of sweat on the back of the old boy's neck. He's really working at it, getting his money's worth. I didn't realize they paid these guys that well that he can afford this. Or maybe this one is off the cuff from her, in exchange for a ride downtown. No, she can't give it away for the equivalent of $1.85, can she? In exchange for a monthly bus pass? That's more likely. I'm witness to a simple exchange of services here.

I can't stand this any more.

"Hey, excuse me."

His ass still pumps. No sign of life from her.

"Mr. Bus Driver. Hey!"

This time he turns his head.

"What the fuck do you want?"

I can't believe this. The dude just doesn't care that I'm watching him have sex on his bus. He's obviously not shy and must have a kick-ass union to boot he feels this secure in his job.

I can't talk to the guy like this. Or maybe I can. I traipsed all the way up here.

"Uhhhmm . . . I'm late for work."

He looks back at me again, his face a bit more strained.

"Yeah?" he grunts.

"I gotta get to work. You gotta get this bus in gear."

The conversation seems to have roused the woman. She peers out from beneath him. Her face is all pasted up: mascara, rouge, baby-blue eye shadow. I can't tell if she's twenty-five or fifty-five. She looks to be a working girl, though. Must be—she, too, is unbothered by my intrusion.

I point down the street. "You're late . . ."

He slows down a bit. "No chance. I know the schedule. And besides, you ain't my boss."

Then he pushes hard against her. She groans.

"I thought the general public *was* your boss," I fire back.

"Fuck that cliché."

I pause for a second and then start again: "But I called Bus Check . . . It said . . ."

The woman barks at me from under him.

"Just let him finish, asshole."

I'm losing my nerve. These are two tough customers. They can argue and fuck at the same time.

I look at the driver in his rumpled uniform. "But Bus Check said . . ."

He turns and glares at me one last time. "Will you please just piss off! Can't you see I'm busy? Get the hell off my bus!"

I think this does it for him. He lets out a gasp and crumbles on top of the woman. She sighs, relieved that it's over.

That's it, I've had it. I'm not waiting around for their post-coital exchange. This is too weird—even for the bus, even for Hamilton.

I beat it down the steps of the bus. Push through the glass doors again. I think about recording the number of the bus, making a complaint. But I doubt that'll have any effect. Instead, I sprint home to call a cab. There's no way I want this HSR driver taking me anywhere tonight. I'll be late for work but I can sort that out later. My supervisor will have to believe this story. No way I could ever make it up.

» » »

Job Action

Kerwin sticks me running with Duguay's crew. I climb into the garbage truck. The driver, a guy I've never worked with, flips through the *Toronto Sun* while drinking from a Thermos lid. It doesn't smell like coffee. He reaches under the seat and pulls up a bottle of rye. He tops himself up. Then looks over at me.

"Drink?"

"Bit early."

"Fuck that. Never too early. Never too late."

He's got a point. "Sure. Pass it over."

He gives me the bottle. I take a drink and cringe. It's 6:45 in the morning.

"Why you drinking out of a cup?"

"Old habit. Used to drink coffee with my rye. Now it's just rye in the morning."

I nod and pass him back the bottle.

Duguay stands next to the truck. He's buying weed off Jeff Smith. I've worked with Duguay a few times before. He's the garbage yard's resident lunatic. He's part garbageman, part drunk, part biker, part criminal. But he's fast, one of the fastest. I've seen him run up and down streets for seven hours straight throwing tonnes of garbage. The drugs help. But normally it's speed. I've never seen Duguay buy dope off Smith at the beginning of a shift. Usually he saves the spliffs for after work, to bring him back down. Something's up.

I turn to the driver. "Why's Duguay buying pot this early? He doesn't usually think that far ahead."

"Duguay's not thinking ahead. He's getting ready to party early."

"Eh? What's up? We not working today?"

"Not like fuckn usual. You ain't heard?"

"Heard what?"

"Negotiations broke off last night. We're heading for a fuckn strike this shit don't get sorted out in the next 48 hours. We're gonna give the bosses a fuckn taste today with some job action. A little slowdown, my friend."

"Explains Duguay's pot. How do you know all this?"

"Everyone knows. Get your fuckn head out of your ass. Smith's on the Local executive."

I look at the scraggly guy selling herb to Duguay. He doesn't look like leadership material, but what do I know.

Duguay pockets the weed and climbs into the truck. He looks me up and down, then says, "Hey, student. Hope you're ready to party."

I shrug. The driver puts the truck in gear and away we go.

» » »

Duguay rolls joints like a pro as the truck rumbles along Barton Street toward the west end. He puts about a dozen joints in his pack of smokes.

When we get to the corner of King Street and Paradise Road, the driver turns north toward Glen Road. Duguay sparks a spliff. We sit in the truck. He takes a hit and then passes it around. Garbagemen always share. I've learned it's really impolite to refuse; it just isn't done, it doesn't matter what time of day it is.

We finish the joint and Duguay says, "Time for work, student."

We're on Glen Road, a quiet, west-end residential street.

"Just do every second or third fuckn stop," Duguay says, pulling on his gloves. "And take your fuckn time. No running today."

I do what he says. I've never seen Duguay this relaxed. Normally, he's nuts to attack the garbage, slay it like a dragon and chuck it into the truck. It's partly the weed but he's really mellow now. It takes us about half-an-hour to do Glen Road, a street that usually takes five minutes.

We turn onto Longwood and Duguay decides it's time for a break. He sits on the curb and stares at his boots. The truck idles, the driver inside picking his nose. I lean against the truck waiting for Duguay.

A car stops beside us and a woman rolls down the window of her air-conditioned vehicle.

"You missed my house," she says.

Duguay looks at her but doesn't say anything.

"Excuse me, but you missed my house," she tries again. "My garbage is still *sitting* in front of my house." She has a really annoying tone.

"Didn't miss nothing," Duguay mumbles.

"What was that?"

Duguay snickers and shakes his head. Then he stands up. He looks like a bear, standing tall, expressionless, contemplating whether to charge and rip this woman's head from her shoulders or lazily slouch back into the forest to gather some berries.

The woman barks, "You missed my house. I pay my taxes. I can tell you what to do."

I hold my breath at that old line. It's going to set Duguay off. I picture him tearing her head off and tossing it in the hopper while her headless body writhes and squirms in the driver's seat, blood splattering the interior of her expensive car. Duguay doesn't take orders from anyone, especially women in imported, air-conditioned cars on their way to some snotty job. He's got a ledger in his head where he tabulates these things and he exacts revenge like only a garbageman can. But, amazingly, he's still chilled out, staring blankly at the woman.

"I'm tellin' yah, lady, we didn't miss your house."

The woman picks up a cell phone. "You give me your name, Mister. I'll call downtown and get your lazy ass fired."

I can't believe she's talking to him like this. How stupid is she? She has no idea who she's dealing with. She could be headless in seconds.

Then Duguay walks over to the car. A few neighbours stick their noses out their front doors, snooping at the commotion.

"Let me in, you can fuckn drive me downtown," Duguay says, reaching for the passenger door.

The woman shrieks and throws her cell at him. She jams the car into gear and peels away, tearing the passenger door handle from Duguay's grasp. He stands there and laughs, watching her speed down the street, spooked, her head still in place but getting smaller and smaller as she accelerates away.

Duguay turns to me. "Time for a drink, student."

We hop back up into the cab. All the dithering neighbours scurry back into their houses.

》 》 》

It's an old garbageman's trick. Change your run at 7:30 in the morning to set the citizens panicking. The idea is to drive along a street you normally do late in the morning, where the citizens are complacent, their garbage not out yet. Then charge the hopper and make noise. The unprepared citizens come running like rats after the Pied Piper. We're looking for yummy mummies in nightdresses and pyjamas. They spill out their front doors, breasts swaying as they madly try and get their garbage to the curb. Cheap thrills, but what else have we got on this shitty job?

Duguay says, "Take a run on Homewood Avenue. See if we can't get us some titty action."

The driver grunts and away we go. Juvenile stuff, but what the hell. The results aren't great. Instead of yummy mummies we get a couple of old bags with their knockers down by their knees, tugging at battered metal cans. Duguay snorts and tells the driver to move on. He waves to the grannies. One of them gives him that Italian cursing gesture; her fingers to her chin and then sprung forward. Duguay laughs. Then he turns to the driver. "Let's go check out your old lady, then."

We're down on Stinson Street, Tuesday work. We've got no business here today. But we're fucking around. Everything is out the window. The driver stops the truck in an alley next to a shitty, four-storey apartment building. There's a small side yard beside the building, next to the alley. A couple of legless couches butt up against the building. An old, toothless guy sits on the building's cement stairs, sucking a smoke. He eyes us suspiciously and then walks away, down Stinson Street.

The driver hits the horn. From a window on the second floor, a woman with dirty blonde hair sticks her head out. She smiles and waves. She's also missing teeth. Must be something in the water in this part of town. She disappears for a second and then comes back. Now she has a hairbrush. She pulls it through her tangles, smiling her Bobby Clarke smile. Duguay laughs and lights a cigarette. The driver checks himself in the cab's side mirror, then hops out. He sits on one of the couches. Duguay follows. I stand around, wondering where this is headed. Then the woman appears out the front door of the building. She's got a twelve of Labatt's Blue under her arm. Her hair's a little less messy, but she's still rough-looking. Pink sweat pants with stains all over them. A Tiger-Cats T-shirt that's way too small for her. She's not wearing a bra. Her tits veer out, point more toward the ground than straight ahead. Bunny slippers, more grey than white. She pulls a cigarette from behind her ear. The driver stands and lights it.

"Thanks, deary."

He steps closer to her and pulls her in, mashing her tits against his belly. Then without a word, they go into the apartment building.

Duguay kicks back on one of the grubby couches and cracks a beer. He tosses me one. A little while later, a couple boys—maybe four and six years old—come out the building's front door. The older one snaps at Duguay, "My mom said you'd watch us."

Duguay doesn't say anything. He stands, picks one kid up under each arm and takes them to the truck. He tosses them in the cab and slams the door. "Don't get out. Play in there." It's not the best playpen. I think about the empties, the skin mags, the Sunshine girls taped up. They've likely seen worse.

Fifteen minutes later, it's Duguay's turn. The driver plunks down on the couch with a satisfied sigh and grabs a beer. I see where this is headed. Remember, garbagemen always share. I finish my beer and reach for another. The driver smiles at me and we clink bottles. Solidarity, brother.

» » »

An hour later, we're back on the streets. We're all pretty much sloshed and heading to the incinerator, even though we've got less than half a load on. The guy at the weigh-scales looks at us queerly when the reading comes in at just over four tonnes. But he waves us through. We dump and head back out.

I'm starting to feel woozy after all the fun and games this morning. I reach for my knapsack to get my lunch. I offer sandwiches but the driver and Duguay decline. Duguay gives me a look that says eating is a stupid idea right now.

The driver says to Duguay. "I'm heading home. Not feeling up to any more of this."

Duguay shrugs and looks out the window. "Pussy," he says under his breath.

We stop in front of a house near the corner of Cannon and Wentworth. The driver gets out and staggers away into a rundown place. Duguay gets out, walks round to the driver's side and climbs in. I know he's not licensed to drive, that he's classified as a general labourer only, but it comes as no surprise when he jams the truck into gear and drives away, back toward the west end.

When we get to Strathcona Avenue he says, "You throw what you want. I'll drive. Hang on. I drive fast."

No shit, I think, taking my life in my hands as I get out. But despite all the pot and booze, Duguay does pretty well. We finish off Strathcona, then Head Street and part of Dundurn Street North. Then a City truck pulls up, the first we've seen all day. Kerwin. I recognize his shit-eating grin from a mile away. He pulls up beside Duguay. I take the opportunity and crash under a scrubby tree on a small lawn. A dog growls at me from behind a chain-link fence, but I don't care. I listen to Kerwin and Duguay argue as I try and sleep. Then Duguay blares the horn. I go over to the truck.

"Hop in. Gotta go pick up a man."

Kerwin's gone. Duguay says, "Kerwin don't like us working short. Says I'm not supposed to drive. Says it's okay to drive and pick up a man. Stupid fuckn asshole. I'll show him what he can do with his fuckn orders."

I don't say anything. It's just past one o'clock. I slouch down in the seat and close my eyes. I hear Duguay spark his lighter, then smell weed as he pulls the truck away from the curb.

» » »

Ten minutes later we're in the District Two yard, just off Barton Street next to the jail. Duguay honks. This skinny guy with slicked back hair gets up off a bench. He grabs a small cooler, picks up his green City of Hamilton jacket, and heads to the driver's side. Duguay doesn't get out.

"Other side," he barks.

The guy looks up blankly, then says, "I'm the driver. Your foreman was just here. Said so." He's got a nasally voice, squeaky and irritating, like the woman who bitched at us this morning about her garbage.

"Fuck that," is all Duguay says.

I get out and the Districts guy climbs in the middle. I can tell things are going to turn ugly, that Duguay will show him no mercy. Garbage guys have no use for District workers. They consider the District guys soft, lazy—the true City-worker, dog-fucker cliché. On the other hand, garbage is like the City workers' nuthouse. You have to be harder and crazier than the slackers in the Districts with their bullshit, stand-around jobs.

In the truck, Duguay goes, "Name?"

"Frank."

"Frank fuckn what?"

"Frank Short."

"You smoke, Frank Short?"

"Yeah. Why?"

"Fuck that and answer the question."

"I just did answer."

Then Frank pulls a deck of smokes from his jacket. He takes out two butts, offering one to Duguay. He might be all right after all. But Duguay's not appeased. He takes Frank's cigarette and puts it behind his ear. Then, still sitting in the District Two yard, Duguay takes out what must be joint number ten of the day, lights it, sucks deeply, blows smoke and passes it to Frank. It's a test. And Frank fails. He sputters something incoherent and holds his palms up like Duguay is offering cyanide-spiked Kool-Aid. I can't believe it. What a fuck-up. What a pussy. No respect for the garbageman's code. Duguay is going to eat this dude alive. He stares at Frank, then pushes the joint toward me. I do the honourable thing: take it and have a hit, then pass it back to Duguay. He puts the spliff between his lips, snarls something while looking straight ahead and drives back out to Barton Street.

Duguay pulls over ten minutes later at the corner of

York and Locke. He turns to Frank. "Here's how this is gonna work. Me and the student here done enough work for the day. You're way behind. You're gonna do a decent day's work for a fuckn change. Get your ass out there and don't come back till I tells you to."

Frank is freaked. Duguay is back looking like an angry bear. So Frank gets out, timidly puts on his gloves and starts picking up bags. He's slow at first. Duguay leans on the horn and yells at him to hurry up. In the cab, me and Duguay smoke dope and listen to Aerosmith. We go up Locke to King, making sure Frank hits every stop. No more slowdown for now. Half-an-hour into it, Frank's ready to collapse. He jumps on the back of the truck at King. Duguay peels around the corner and almost loses him. I check the side mirror. Frank looks panic-stricken. Duguay fucks with him more. He drives by the stops on King—he hits 50, 60 kilometres per hour, our man still on the back. Duguay turns left at Dundurn and drives toward Main Street. He pulls the same trick, driving all the way up to Queen Street with Frank bobbing and bouncing on the back like a dog being dragged on a leash behind a car. Duguay roars with laughter. I'm a little worried the fucker will tumble into traffic. But finally Duguay stops, just east of Hess. He hits the horn, signals out the window and Frank staggers up to the cab. He gets in, panting.

"What the fuck, you nearly killed me out there."

Duguay looks at him squarely. "Yeah, sorry 'bout that,

brother. Don't know the route so good. Got a bit lost. Got a bit fucked up. Lemme buy you lunch and make it up to you."

Frank shakes his head and folds his sweaty hands in his lap.

» » »

We're down by Centre Mall, Wednesday work. We pull up next to a grey building and Duguay gets out. He chucks open a bin and starts throwing garbage like a maniac. Bags fly into the hopper. He looks at me for half a second. I go over and charge the hopper. Duguay keeps throwing. Frank stands around looking confused. Then a guy comes out of the building. He barks something at Duguay but I don't catch it. I read the sign on the building—Sunshine Bakery—and figure it out. This is part of Fast Feet Freddy Paterson's run—his Wednesday meal ticket. The bakery gives the men free range at the buffet in exchange for preferential treatment. It's another garbageman's trick, a form of extortion. The men promise to do a top-notch job, not to drop any food waste into the alley or out back of the restaurant. In doing so, the rats are kept at bay, as is the City health inspector. But as hard as Duguay is, I'm surprised he's moving in on Fast Feet's turf. There will be fireworks in the yard tomorrow. He tosses all fifty bags neatly into the hopper without a crumb hitting the pavement. Then he turns to me and Frank.

"Like I said, lunch is on me. Belly up to the buffet, you dog fuckers."

Inside, Duguay scarfs down chicken cutlets, meat pies, corn, pasta and bread, and then guzzles three cups of coffee. I do my best to eat but I'm feeling nauseous from the booze, drugs, and heat. Frank just nibbles at a bun and some cheese like a fucking imbecile. Duguay, chewing on a butter tart, jumps up and summons us to the truck. Then it's off to the Running Pump, a biker bar in the North End. Tuesday work. We do their garbage and suck back free beer by the truck. Frank still abstains. It's about three o'clock. I'm completely hammered, barely able to stand. Duguay slaps my back and grabs Frank by the scruff of his T-shirt. He steers us into the Pump. We shoot pool badly for an hour. Me and Duguay drink beer and rye. Frank finally gives in and sips a Coors Light. A couple Monday-afternoon sluts gravitate to Duguay. He's in fine form now, wasted but fully fuelled-up, on his game. He disappears with both sluts for five minutes. When he comes back, he gives me a drunken come-hither gesture with a grubby finger and then shoves me into the arms and breasts of the two women. They take me out by the truck. One of them blows me while the other plays with my hair and coos in my ear. They act like porn stars— exaggerated puckers, tits thrust out, getting me off and then moving on. After, I pass out in the truck, unable to take any more.

I come to when Duguay roars the engine to life. Instead of Frank, the two sluts are in the cab next to me. One flips through a skin mag, giggling. The other sucks on a smoke, banging her head to Aerosmith. We tear away from the Pump. Duguay turns east onto Burlington Street and leans on the gas. He hits sixty, seventy klicks. He veers between cars and transports, whooping madly, the truck listing like a boat in a storm. The two women love it and join in the ruckus, party-howling and pumping the air with their fists. I pray we don't crash.

Then, Jeff Smith appears in a City pickup, a supervisor's truck. He's doing about eighty klicks trying to catch us. He's got the siren going, something I've never seen before. I always wondered what the sirens were for. Pulling over insane garbage truck drivers, I guess. Smith's likely out of his head as well. How did he get his hands on that vehicle? What supervisor is in debt to him for weed so badly he handed over the keys to his truck?

Duguay spots Smith in the side mirror and stops the truck in the middle of Burlington Street. He's blocking two lanes. Why should he care at this point what laws he breaks. Smith stops next to him. He jumps out and gives the finger to various drivers who honk and holler. He climbs up on the driver's side door.

"Wanted you to be the first to know."

He's talking to Duguay, not to me. Smith's so messed up, he doesn't notice the women.

"Bosses are gonna settle. I just come from a meeting downtown."

I want to laugh. I mean, look at this guy; he's stoned, drunk, reeks of garbage, hasn't shaved or bathed for a week and he's talking about a meeting downtown. Organized labour, you gotta love it.

Duguay says, "So, what's up?"

"They're gonna fuckn settle. Give us all we asked for. They can't handle a garbage strike in the middle of summer. I took some fuckn suit out for a drive. Showed him all the piles rotting on the curb. Talked to him about rats. Talked to him about the fuckn diseases. Showed him some fuckn maggots up close on stinking piles of garbage. Let him get a good, long sniff. Told him the whole city would stink like that about two days into the strike. The stupid fucker bought it. He looked spooked. The fucker's likely never worked a real day in his life for the City but there he is telling me what's what. Dumb cunt. I showed him. Our action worked, no fuckn doubt."

Duguay scoffs, "No strike? And I was just startin' to have some fun."

"No reason for that to stop, brother. Point is, we got these fuckers by the balls now."

Smith jumps down and gets back in the City pickup. Duguay sits there letting it sink in. He pulls a joint out of his pack of smokes. He lights it up and offers it to me. I take a hit and pass the joint back to Duguay. He tells the women to get out. They groan in synch, climb out and start walking west on Burlington Street. The party's over.

Then Duguay puts the truck in gear and we head to the incinerator. We have to dump this load, then go back out and finish the work we've fucked around with all day. It'll take us past dark. We'll get paid overtime. It's all part of our greater victory, our job action. The overtime is added consolation for selling your soul for a lousy paycheque to keep the salivating dogs away.

» » »

The next morning I bump into Duguay coming into the yard from the bus. I'm badly hung over. So is he. Duguay stops me for a second. He looks me over, making sure he has the right man. "Sorry 'bout the erratic driving," he says after a bit. I give my head a shake. The alcohol and drugs linger in my system so I'm not sure I heard him right. Then Duguay shuffles off, looking sort of depressed. I guess I heard him right. Two things strike me: Duguay apologized and he used the word erratic. Amazing. Absolutely fuckn amazing. This job blows my mind every day.

» » »

The Summer of No Love

I first met her after her appointment with a psychiatrist. A mutual friend—Kathy—had set us up. Kathy was tired of me trying to fuck her. She was engaged to be married at the end of the summer. She felt threatened by me or was fed up or both. We'd messed around a bit; she'd jerked me off a few times but that was it. Understandably, Kathy wanted rid of me so she pawned me off on her nutty friend. I was only told that her friend was beautiful and eager—a good combination. I was willing to take my chances with her unstable mental state. I used to work as a custodian at a psychiatric hospital; I was used to nutcases. But whatever was wrong with her upstairs didn't really enter into the equation for me. The state I was in, it wasn't her mind I was after.

I waited for her appointment to be over. I stood in the foyer of the big hospital with my hands in the pockets of my shorts, checking out the nurses coming and going. The air was cool inside—a break from the smothering July heat.

Eventually, she showed. She came to me slowly, warily, her head tilted to one side. She looked like she might topple over. She wore short shorts that bunched at her crotch. Her legs were too fat; doughy thighs and calves. I could tell she'd never done anything athletic in her life. She wore a small, tight T-shirt. Breasts medium-sized but pointy. A bit of a belly. Her hair was shoulder length and jet-black. A purse slung over one shoulder. Sandals. Big dark eyes, supple lips and an ethnic moustache in need of a trim. She was pretty at a certain angle but not beautiful, as was advertised.

"You're Steven?"

"Yeah. Hi."

"Kathy described you perfectly." She smiled.

"Yeah, you too," I said. I thought it best to lie from the start.

She didn't want to shake my hand when I offered it. Instead, she wanted me to kiss her hand, which seemed ridiculous in the foyer of a sterile, purple-carpeted hospital. But I did. And later—after four or five drinks at her place—I kissed her supple lips, her dark eyes and her pointy breasts. She tried to push my head down further to kiss her cunt but we'd only just met—that would have to wait. She had no similar qualms about sucking my cock. I shot my wad into her mouth. She swallowed it whole and tried to suck out more. I was impressed by her enthusiasm and drawn to her sluttishness. She was definitely eager, as advertised.

She smoked a cigarette in her small basement apartment. We had another drink, then she blew me again.

At the door to her flat when I was leaving she told me she was going to bed to masturbate until she fell asleep. She said she did that every night. I wasn't sure if she said this to shock me or entice me to spend the night. But we'd only just met so I didn't say anything and didn't kiss her goodnight. I left her there at the threshold leaning against the doorframe.

》 》 》

She called me the next afternoon to say she had just finished taking a long, hot bath, despite the heatwave. She told me how she had soaked in the bath for more than an hour. She had lathered herself with soap, covering every square centimetre of her flesh. She told me how she had stuck a dildo up her cunt in the bath, hot water sloshing around her clean body as she slipped the dildo slowly in and out. Did I want to come over? she asked. I told her I'd be there in twenty minutes but didn't show for more than three hours.

The door was unlocked when I got there so I let myself in after knocking twice. She was slouched in a grubby beanbag chair in her small sitting room—one of only two pieces of furniture in the room. There was also an end table that sat at the end of nothing across the room from the beanbag chair. Her eyes were glazed from drugs. I recalled her psychiatric appointment. She said nothing about it the night before. I had no idea what her condition was and wasn't too concerned about it. She just sat back in the filthy beanbag chair staring at me. I wasn't sure she recognized me. When she didn't get out of the beanbag chair, I went over, took off my shorts and underwear, straddled her face and stuck my semi-stiff prick in her face. She didn't blink. It might have been the meds, might have been her natural state, but whatever it was she blew me with indifferent, mechanical precision before even saying hello. After, she didn't ask why I was more than three hours late.

Then she snapped out of it and told me she was hungry. She asked could I go out and get us something. She said she had no money and that there was nothing to eat in her kitchen. All she had was booze and tea. I asked, did she want to come with me? We could eat out. She said no. Said she was going to take another bath—this one cold.

She would wait in the bath until I got back with the food.

I took my time. I stopped at a bar for a beer. That only made me want more so I stopped at the beer store and got a six-pack. I drove up and down a strip of fast food joints with a beer open at my crotch. I eventually settled on pizza.

When I got back to her place she was asleep in the tub. The water was cold around her. She could have been dead, it was that cold. I opened a beer, sat on the toilet seat cover and watched her for a while. She breathed very slowly. Then I knocked my beer bottle against the side of the tub and she woke up groggily. She adjusted herself and looked at me. She didn't startle. Then she climbed out of the cold water and her entire body pursed up—her flesh goosebumped, her breasts shrunk into cold hard mounds. I didn't reach for a towel. Instead I grabbed her left tit, squeezing and twisting the iron-like nipple. She barely reacted. So I stroked her cold ass with my other hand, then slid it up and down her fat thigh. She started to shake and tremble and then turned to offer me a head-on look at her cunt. I took a drink of my beer and examined her shrivelled pussy from where I sat on the toilet. It was right at eye level.

"Touch me there, it's stone cold," she said.

I looked up at her face. I put the beer bottle to my lips and shook my head back and forth. I took the bottle away and said, "You do it you want it touched so badly."

She looked disappointed and her eyes drifted away from mine. She stood still, unsure what to do. Her indecisiveness pissed me off so I threw her a towel, told her to dry off and go lie on her bed. I undressed in the bathroom and stroked my cock hard. I put on a condom and then fucked her for the first time. Despite the layer of latex and my thrusts, she was right: her cunt was stone cold. It took ages to warm up. But she came around after a while and started to match my rhythm. I was bothered by her exaggerated moans but was still able to knock off a load and then roll away from her.

I sat at the end of her bed, drank beer and ate pizza.

"Pizza? You got pizza?" she asked when she sat up. She sounded disgusted by it, like pizza was beneath her. She didn't eat.

More for me, I thought and ate on. She lay back and fell asleep naked, legs parted, her pink pussy wide open and pointed at me, as if it was keeping an eye on me, didn't trust me.

When I'd eaten enough, I kissed her on the forehead, left her asleep and quietly backed out of the room.

» » »

She called the next day at six o'clock in the morning.

"What the fuck are you doing? I was sound asleep."

She had no idea what I was talking about. She thought

it was six o'clock at night. She said her basement flat confused her. I told her to jerk herself off and go back to sleep. Then I felt bad for lashing out at her so I promised to come by later with wine and roses. She laughed and hung up without saying goodbye.

» » »

I did like I said I was going to do. I bought three bottles of expensive wine and a dozen roses. It was a stupid cliché gift for a stupid cliché girl. She nearly wet herself she was so excited.

"No one's ever done this for me before."

"That so?"

"Yeah, you're the first. You're so sweet. I can't believe it. For me, really?"

"Yeah, of course. Who else?"

She didn't have an opener. I pushed the cork down in the bottle and we drank red wine out of tea cups on her bed. Two cups and she was drunk. She giggled and wriggled and spilled her wine. It left red splotches on her white sheets. It gave me an idea. I plucked petals from the red roses and laid them across the bed. I saved one rose that I clamped between my teeth. More cliché. But she came at me, tore the rose from my mouth and cast it aside. Then she lay back on the rose petals and began to writhe around. I laughed at her and drank my wine. She yelped.

She'd rolled onto the stem of the rose and cut herself on a thorn. Her fat thigh was bleeding. Her dark eyes watered and it looked like she was going to cry. Something came over me. I leaned forward and sucked her wound. She winced at first but then found something sensual in it and began again with the moaning. My prick got hard. She wanted to suck me off but I wasn't letting go of my lip grip on her leg and the angle didn't allow her near my cock, so she masturbated instead. I think she came. I took my mouth away from her cut and rubbed my cock there instead until I spunked on her wound. That dreamy, drugged look came over her face again and she crashed back into the rose petals and fell instantly asleep. Sleeping beauty, sort of.

I finished the open bottle of wine, grabbed the two unopened ones and left.

» » »

She surprised me a couple of days later when she telephoned to say she wanted go out with some friends. She wanted me to come along. As far as I could tell, she hadn't left her flat since our first "date" after her visit to the shrink. I wondered whether her problem was agoraphobia but then dismissed it. She said she was going to hook up with a bunch of her old friends from high school at some bar I'd never heard of in the east end. It sounded boring but harmless. I was feeling claustrophobic hanging out in her small, basement apartment and figured I could use a change of scenery with her.

Her friends were boring. The guys talked about cars and jobs. The girls talked about going to Toronto to see a show, something to do with Abba. The girls quizzed me and tried to expose me for something. It was pointless. The guys mostly ignored me. They were old boyfriends; imbeciles latched onto their dull and semi-dumb girlfriends.

I wanted to tell the girls that she gave great head but they probably knew already. Their boyfriends probably knew too. The way she sucked cock, she had a past that would be common knowledge. I wanted to tell them that I hadn't seen her eat since I'd known her. That I feared she almost never left her flat. That she had a fucking end table that just sat there doing nothing in her dreary basement flat. But they probably already knew all of this or didn't care. It was me they were trying to root out. So I told lies about my line of work. Then I got bored and went to the bar to drink alone. One of the guys tried to befriend me there later but I gave him the cold shoulder. I waited and waited and finally she came over.

"You're not being very social. You're not being very polite."

"I've done enough. They're vultures picking over my corpse."

"Don't be so dramatic. Don't exaggerate."

"Yeah, enough then. You're right. Come fuck me in the can and then let's get the hell out of here."

I took her into a stall and spun her around. She was wearing a skirt. I reached up and pulled her panties down below her knees. She braced herself by leaning forward above the toilet and placing her hands on the wall. She looked like she was trying to pee standing up. I pumped her for a minute or two and then came. She wheeled around, kissed me hard and squeezed my balls. I pushed her away and she sat down hard on the toilet. Again she looked disappointed. Again she looked like she might cry, sitting there disconsolate on the toilet with her panties down. Is that how she looked when she shitted? I didn't know. I'd never seen her eat, let alone shit.

I reached down and raised her chin. I leaned forward and kissed her slowly. Then I reached down and stuck two fingers up her snatch. She pulled away and glared at me.

"Now you want to touch me? In a fucking toilet stall?"

I heard the door to the washroom open. She recognized the voices: two of the lughead boyfriends. Her demeanour changed.

"Go on," she called out loudly. "Stick two fingers, three fingers, four—stick your whole hand up my pussy if you want to touch me like that."

There was silence at the urinals. She moaned and grabbed my hand. I did as she commanded and got four fingers in.

"More," she hollered but it was tough working in cramped quarters.

"Fuck it, then," I said, quietly. I pulled my fingers out and backed away from her.

She started jerking herself off madly. She glared at me the entire time. The boyfriends scampered out without a word. She came, then put a palm in the centre of my chest and pushed me away. She left the washroom.

When I got to the bar, she was propped on a stool chatting up the bartender, content to ignore me. I said nothing. I went to the waitress who had been serving us. I put fifty bucks on her tray then walked out. I drove away alone. Our first fight. I didn't cry.

» » »

I called her the next afternoon. She was surprised to hear from me and started apologizing.

I didn't want to hear it. I cut her off. "Did you fuck the bartender?"

"What? What are you talking about?"

"You sucked his cock then?"

"You're not serious. What're you talking about? We're . . ."

"So it's yes then? Because you haven't said no."

"Listen, you left and you pissed me off and . . ."

"So it's yes? Say it. Say it if it is. I don't really care. I'm not surprised. You think you can shock me but you don't know me at all. So just fucking say it. No, wait. Say it to me in person."

She tried to stammer a reply but I was already hanging up the phone.

» » »

When I got to her place she was crying. There was a bottle of pills on her end table. Finally, she had put it to use. The bottle sat near the edge of the table, about to fall. A couple pills had spilled out. I picked up the bottle: Elavil, an anti-depressant.

"You shouldn't have left me there alone," she blubbered. "You just left. You didn't say goodbye. I thought you were gone for good."

"So you sucked the bartender's cock instead? Fuck, sounds like you were really broken up about us."

"You don't understand. I need reassurance. My doctor says and my friends say—"

"Fuck that. You just like to suck cock. You need to. It helps you sleep at night or something, right?"

"You're a pig."

"Maybe, but I'm getting closer to the truth now. It's that and these drugs. Reassurance. Reassurance my fucking ass. You need a cock as much as you need these meds. Right?"

She just wheezed and blew her nose. She turned away from me and collapsed on the beanbag chair. She pulled herself into the foetal position. I stood over her.

"You want me to stay or go?"

She said something I couldn't hear.

"Speak up. Stay or go?"

"Stay, of course. Stay. Fuck. Please."

"Beg me."

"What?"

She started to come to life. She came out of the foetal position and turned to face me.

"You heard me. Beg me to stay."

"You're not serious."

"You don't and I go and that's the end of it."

She crawled out of the beanbag chair and kneeled at my feet. She tried to reach up for my cock but I wasn't having it, not now.

"That's not what I said to do. I said beg. Beg me to stay. Do it or I'm outa here."

She propped herself on her knees. She pulled her black hair out of her face and looked up at me. She managed, "Stay."

I made like I was turning to leave. She grabbed my leg and wrapped her arms around me. "Stay! Please, stay."

"More."

"Fuck. I beg you. I beg you to stay."

"Beg. I want you to actually beg."

She looked a bit hurt and worried. Then she sat back on her haunches and folded her hands in front of her like a little girl praying. She closed her eyes and then opened them, batting her eyes at me. More cliché. It was perfect.

"More."

She puckered her lips behind her folded hands. "Please stay, oh please stay. I can't live without you. I couldn't bear it. Please."

"Enough of the shit. Beg me with your eyes, your body."

She leaned forward, her hair brushing my legs. She lowered her face to my feet. Her nose was right down by the ground. I shuffled my feet, urging her to look up. Her eyes were dark pools. She was on the verge of weeping. She tilted her head and begged me with her eyes.

"Okay. Enough. Get up on your knees."

I was disappointed with the begging. I thought I'd get more of a charge out of humiliating her like that. So I opened my pants. She blew me and then fell back asleep in the beanbag chair.

» » »

She called me the next afternoon.

"You weren't very nice to me yesterday."

"Hey, you were the one out sucking another guy's cock."

"I never said that."
"You didn't have to."
"You were mean, vicious. Mean and vicious."
"And?"
She didn't say anything else.

» » »

I called three days later to see if she wanted to go out. She was home in bed reading a book, a romance novel. Her bedroom was cluttered with them. She read at least one a day and then tossed them aside like the morning paper.
"Why don't you come over here instead?"
"That's all we do."
"Yeah but you don't seem to mind. You seem to enjoy yourself while you're here."
She had a point.
"Come over and ravish me," she said and then laughed.
The word was packed with possibility.
"I'll be over in twenty minutes."
I was there in less than twenty minutes. Again the door was open. In I went. Not a sound. There were no pills spilled anywhere. I stepped through the sitting room to her bedroom. She wasn't there. Not in the tiny bathroom either. That only left the kitchen. I'd never seen her in the kitchen. But I checked. She was standing stock still over a sink of soapy suds and dishes. She didn't turn to

acknowledge me. She wore a skirt and a short, cropped T-shirt with an apron laced around her waist. No shoes. I took it all in. Her hair looked clean and well-brushed. Her dark skin looked radiant under the crappy fluorescent lights.

I took two steps over and pushed her forward against the counter.

"Don't move."

I undid the apron and tossed it aside. I lifted her skirt. I licked two fingers and then stuck them in. I jammed them in as far as they would go, then rotated them round and round to loosen her up, to make room. I pushed her legs further apart. I grabbed at her ass. I slapped it. Slapped it hard. I pushed her feet apart. I stood behind her and pressed my cock into her ass cheeks. She winced. I rubbed my cock up and down her ass crack. She tensed. Then I pushed my cock lower and stuffed it in. She splashed in the dishwater as she braced herself. I fucked her like that. I pushed her forward, her pelvis pressed against the counter top. Water sloshed around in the sink. She started making noises so I put one hand over her mouth. I pushed her head forward. I fucked her this way, then came and stepped away.

"Don't move. I still don't want you to move."

I sat at the only chair in her small kitchen. I watched my semen run down her leg. I grabbed a tea towel and threw it at her. Then I turned and left.

»   »   »

Afterward I felt pathetic. I felt pathetic for myself and for her. The relationship was starting to lose its lustre. At the time, raping her in her kitchen seemed a good charge but it was over so fast I wasn't sure what the bother was. True, it wasn't pure rape—she had invited me over for it, had set it up. She was as compliant as ever. That was where it was wearing thin. No challenge. She just kept giving in and giving herself up like a cheap whore. I was distracted. It had been about five weeks. Summer was winding down, not that the autumn would bring any major changes for me.

I decided I'd had enough. That was when she really started to beg me.

»   »   »

Phone calls at all hours. She took the bus to my place and pounded on the door, but I wouldn't open it. She left me notes. She drew me pictures—sad pictures of her crying under a grey sky, leafless brown trees bowing around her. The drawings were good but I was unmoved. She left dirty messages on my answering machine. That roused me a little. I worried I was going to crack. Time was passing. It was nearly a week since the crap in her kitchen. If she showed up at my door again I might give in. I stayed away from my place when I wasn't working.

After eight days the phone calls, notes and drawings stopped cold. I waited three more days and still nothing. I started to feel guilty, some responsibility for her. I was feeling human and it was all her fault—she'd wakened something in me after all.

I called her place. No answer. Nothing. Her answering machine didn't come on. I fretted but let it go for a few days.

» » »

Later it gnawed at me more. I thought of her depression and her pills. Maybe she'd taken the entire bottle; maybe she'd stopped taking them altogether.

Late on a Thursday night I went to find out. I parked across the street from her small walk-up apartment building. Her basement flat was all lit up. I got out of my car and walked to the sidewalk in front of her place. I stood off to one side to obscure myself. I wasn't there ten seconds before she bounced into her sitting room wearing only panties. Her small, pointy breasts jostled. She had a drink in one hand. Then a guy in boxer shorts appeared and grabbed her around the waist. He might have been one of the boyfriends from the bar that night. I hadn't paid enough attention at the time to be sure. But she pulled away from him playfully, spilling her drink. She fell to the floor giggling before coming up on her knees in the middle of the room. She was all lit up, there for all to see.

It was pathetic. I was pathetic for watching. But she looked happier than me. She looked like her mental state was reasonably solid. I was the one lurking on the dark street staring in her window.

I let it go. I'd seen enough. I'd seen it before. I turned away from her basement flat window, walked back to my car and drove downtown.

》 》 》

Giants

I put my hand inside myself at the Coffee Time counter, junction of Highways 7 and 134. Dig for change to pay for coffee. Tickles a bit. Coins don't quite rattle, clunk more like next to fleshy muscle, the change quieter than in your standard pocket.

I've been driving for a year and a day. It feels that way. From Hamilton, through Toronto's ugly, slithering superhighways, up gasoline alley, Peterborough bypass, to here. A year and a day. No shit. Traffic was bad. The whole way on honeycomb wheels, beeswax tires. Wings made of iron ore. Crushing steel insects as I drove. Asphalt hot even in mid-April. Sun high in the sky. Grey snow melting into puddles of oily black.

Easter Monday. Christ rose yesterday, some say. But I

didn't see him and I was in a cemetery for an hour burying my brother, Christopher. I looked for headstones rolled away, overturned monuments, ripped up sod—evidence of a resurrection. There was none. Just me a doubting Thomas. Saw a couple dozen sombre mourners standing over a great big hole in the semi-thawed earth, all of them fidgeting, shuffling feet, yearning for an end to the uneasy ceremony, wary of death. Me as well. Hands in pockets, then out. Unstuck my boots from slushy muck. Hands through hair. Itch here and there. That's when I found the hole in my side.

Since then the flesh has hardened, become almost scab-like inside, at least near where it opens. First it was gushy; soft and pink like the inside of your mouth, like the inside of a woman. A bit of exposure, bit of cold air, and it's stiffened right up. But not covered over. Warm on the inside, just under what's probably my left lung, above the guts, kidneys. Is the liver in there somewhere? Pancreas? Softer as you get deeper. Bits of lint. I may have lost a dime or two, a few pennies misplaced in my flesh, toured my intestines, to be shit out sideways later, not that I'll notice, probably not. A bit of change, no reason to sift through my excrement. Like those guys who drop quarters into airport urinals to conduct an experiment—who's desperate enough to reach into the piss and pull out twenty-five cents? Not me. Probably the fuckers who fly business class. Or maybe they get the last laugh, passing the quarter on to some grunt shining shoes or schlepping coffee at Tim Hortons.

"Your quarter is moist and smells funny."

"Legal tender, my friend," then a cruel laugh, before heading to the cream and sugar kiosk.

Which is what I need, but not cream, milk—milk and lots of sugar. Got a long drive ahead.

» » »

Two weeks later I stumble out of Masterson's Tavern in Marmora. Two weeks of pickled eggs, beer, darts, farts and trivia. I'm not fit to drive. Not fit for much. I head to Bob's Pizza across the street and down a ways.

Sheila, behind the counter, glares and barks at me, "We don't deliver outa town. Thought you'da known this by now."

One of Sheila's legs is longer than the other. Keeps her mostly miserable.

I come back with, "No, no, I'm here for pick up. Called it in from up the street. Up Masterson's." Then I look over at the bins of flatware. All appears clean.

Sheila blurts, "Masterson's? That hell hole? Nothing but no good ever comes outa there." She fidgets with a bracelet. Picks dead skin off her elbows.

I reach inside myself, pull out a wad of twenties, gangster like. Slip one off.

"Large pizza. Pepperoni. Mushrooms. Pineapple. Like I said on the phone last week."

Sheila scoffs, "This look like the South Pacific?"

"Yeah, Tahiti. Place has Tahiti written all over it." I point at the flatware.

"Stick your arse outside you want Tahiti."

"No pineapple then I guess?"

"No sir."

"Fuckn green peppers then?"

"No can do. All out. And watch your language. You're not in church no more." She gestures up the street toward the tavern. "Those I don't suppose you sing in the choir," she says, then hoots, belly fat jiggling at her apron seams.

I fire back, "Yeah, *He* is risen," very sarcastic like. Then genuflect. Stand and cross myself. Pious look on my face.

"Careful," she says.

"Serious. My saviour and yours."

"Never mind all that. What'd'ya want to drink with the pizza?"

I'm tempted to say wine, red wine, but I don't. "Got Tahiti Treat?"

"Don't get smart."

"Sorry. Apple juice and a coffee."

"I'm on it. All over it. Quick as a bunny."

Away she limps to the ovens, hoppity-plunk. Comes back a few days later with the best pizza you can get west of Montreal.

» » »

Three weeks later by Silver Lake it's the giants that are after me. Has something to do with Christopher. He died young. Pituitary gland exploded. Brain basically drowned in its own juices. Pickled. He grew too quickly. Weed-like. Over eight feet tall when it stopped, when he dropped dead. A long way down, even though he was sitting—more like crouching—by the letter slot waiting for the new Canadian Tire flyer. He was determined to live a long and fruitful life, growing on and on and up and up. Was planning to renovate.

He'd said, "Lotsa giants live fine and dandy, no problems."

I stared up at him. "Christopher you grow out of your clothes after one washing. So there's really no point in doing laundry. Just wear your trousers four days, then throw them out and buy a new pair."

"It's gonna get expensive."

"Got that fuckn right." I gave him a jar of pickled red peppers. Can't stomach the things myself. All red and slippery and flaccid. Look like someone's insides served on a dish. Christopher gobbled them up. Peered down at me.

"You're jealous. You've got short-man's disease."

He had a point but I wasn't giving an inch, not to a freak of nature, brother or not.

"Not what we're here to talk about Christopher."

"Yeah, then what are we here to talk about?"

He had me there, have to admit it. To distract him, I asked if he'd made coffee. He pointed down the corridor toward his kitchen. "Fresh pot. Help yourself."

Christopher's coffin was long as an SUV. Ten pallbearers, me included. I got stuck with a corner.

» » »

The hole in my side itches. I think it's infected. Maybe stigmata. The ice is just breaking up on Silver Lake. Mid-July now. Long, long winter. I look at my alligator shoes bought at a flea market a week ago, sixty kilometres west of here, back down 7. Sixty dollars lighter. A buck per klick. More twenties off my wad. Paid in cash. No tax. No change, which was important—I suspected intestinal trouble with all those disappearing dimes and coppers. The man at the flea market offered me ten thousand bucks for the hole in my side. Said he knew a man in Madoc who's been looking for exactly what I've got. I ran screaming from the place, new shoes pinching my feet, rubbing the skin raw, threatening pustules.

By the shore of Silver Lake I finger the hole in my side. It's not for sale, my hole. Can't put a price on such things. That guy, that guy at the flea market, there was something wrong with him. I saw the way he looked at me, at my hole. He had more than a monetary transaction in mind. Stick my hand all the way in, feel the softest bit at the bottom, wonder whatever happened to the Centurion who pierced Jesus just so. More likely a regular foot soldier just following orders. That old excuse, even back then. Have to look it up if I ever get to Ottawa.

Before I know it half a dozen giants come crashing out from the lake. Right when I want to pick at the hole—loose the dead skin, taste it, eat the flesh—the giants converge. They stand over me, soaking wet. And it has nothing to do with Christopher. These are old-fashioned giants. Not the Robert Pershing Wadlow type at all, felled by a blister gone terribly wrong. Not like Edouard Beaupre or even Maximinus Thrax. I mean fairy story giants. Big bulbous heads. Meaty arms and hairy legs. Fee-fi-fo-fum. Clubs in arms. But you have to know how to play them, know what they like. Everything—even giants—has a soft spot, an underbelly. I stand, straightening to my nearly six feet. The giants crouch. The whole township stinks of their breath.

Behind me, out on the highway, transport trucks trundle on, oblivious, schedules to keep. In the lake, ice floes jostle in cold water. Cottagers grow impatient with summer's dawdling. Two signs are visible across the highway from where I'm standing: SMALL ENGINE REPAIR: 2 KMS and then a crudely rendered arrow. The other: CLEAN FILL WANTED 842-6344. I finger my hole, ruminatively.

The giants rouse my attention. They're waiting for me,

lake water dripping off hairy frames. I taste sunflower seeds and blood on my tongue. Lift my shirt. Show the giants the hole in my side and before you can say Jack Sprat, in they jump, one at time, into my flesh. It makes a strange slurping sound. They fidget for room. Six or eight of them squeeze in. A murder of giants. A colony. A congregation. I don't know the proper terminology. But in seconds, they're gone.

I'm bloated. Walk slowly to my car. Roll my eyes when I notice the pizza boxes stacked in the backseat. Get in. Start the engine. Put it in gear. Pull up to the highway—my beloved #7. Not sure, for a minute, whether to go east or west. Maybe drive back and see the man at the flea market. I've got half a dozen, maybe more, giants inside my hole. Might make that sale after all.

>> >> >>

Begotten, Not Made

This is how I came to be at the side of the road as the sun came up with my shit-box car idling on the shoulder, hands folded in front of me like an altar boy muttering words dredged from deep in my memory: "I believe in one God, Father, Almighty, Maker of Heaven and Earth and of all things visible and invisible."

It was the fuckn dark that got to me and started me thinking of things visible and invisible. That and disease, drink and her and His one and only son and how the last time I was in that hospital the chaplain nailed my rotting flesh to the wall with questions about destruction, about direction, about culpability.

"What have you done to all those who reached out to help? Where are you going to turn next? Who can you possibly blame now?"

He ranted at me, a preacher mad with love, his heart in the right place, I'll give him that much. I walked away from that institution, spilled my chequing account and bought a 1986 Mazda 626 from a guy named Mort. Car had 264,000 kilometres on it. Started pushin' it toward 300,000. I'm not quite there; this fine, Japanese automobile refuses to quit. I refuse to quit.

I'm headin' back again, drawn in by the lure of a winding, two-lane highway north of Hastings, south of Bancroft. She's here, somewhere. And you can forget the 401. The 401 is for suckers. Can't pray in a service centre Tim Hortons. Halleluiah.

Marmora is a beautiful town that will never be swallowed by any city's encroaching suburbs. With the sun east over Ottawa, with the river babbling beside me, I start with the Nicean Creed again, pickin' up somewhere in the middle: "Who for us men and for our salvation came down from Heaven and was incarnate of the Holy Spirit and the Virgin Mary and became man."

How I remember these words is mind-boggling. Can't remember what I had for supper last night at the Red Dog Inn in Peterborough but I remember the Creed as clear as day. Speaking of which, I remember how I became man and it had something to do with a virgin. Me, not her. So she told me. Patricia. Met at a dance, a Catholic school dance; St. Mary's. A likeness of Christ looked down at us all weary and weepy-eyed from the gymnasium wall while we mashed our groins together, stupid with alcohol, crazy with lust. My cock spitting mad in my pants. My shorts the next morning stiff with dried cum. I'd tagged along with Eug, Jay, Paxton, splitting a case of Old Veranda among us, stubby beer bottles fitted snugly in our teenaged hands, empties tossed into snowbanks, left there till spring.

Patricia. The start of something, no question. She played me like a fuckn violin, her hands wrapped around my neck, throttling me, working me this way and that, purging me of sin. My cock sputtered out its cumly offerings like to some delirious, insatiable god every time I met her, every time I touched her, every time I smelled her, every time I came within ten metres of her sacred body. Or every time her image jammed itself in my head: nights I couldn't sleep, boring bus rides, or any glint of dreary down time; just needed a few minutes, really. Patricia. Always on my mind. Always near at hand. Took matters into my hands, often. More cumly offerings. In total, buckets of the stuff. Enough to fill a fount. The flesh made whole. My whole flesh for her.

I haven't prayed in at least fifteen years. But last night I listened to Nick Cave sing something about raising his hands in supplication while the rain hammers down and I started thinking, why not? What harm can it do? Noah, rain, religion. All the saints I've known. It adds up. Besides, I was alone in my car, the music keeping time with the wipers and not a soul about in the dark, in the stillness of Highway 7, somewhere east of Peterborough.

The remission of sins. That's a good one. That one sticks in the mind the same way roadside gravel grinds into my knees: leaves an impression. I pray by the side of the road. Have I mentioned this? Most guys stop for a piss, cock in hand, stare into farmers' fields, cows ruminating, could care less about a man's micturation. Me, the shoulder is sacred ground. An altar at the cusp of the road. I'm back to it, back to praying, looking Heavenward, searching for inspiration. And God is everywhere, right? Lesson number one all those years ago. Watch what you get up to, the omnipotent one sees all, knows all. The perfect social control scheme: keep us in line with threats of 24/7 surveillance from a ruthless maker, punishing overseer. But damn it, Patricia. Even *He* must have seen she was worthy of my sin, worthy of my spilt seed—amidst the thorns, amidst the stones, amidst the fertile soil where it might take root. Know what I'm on about?

In prayer, next to the bleak highway, from the glove compartment I drew a bottle of rye, holy water, firewater, in lieu of wine; whisky is my sacrament of choice. Who will remit my sins now? Wash them away? As simple as all that; a few muttered words and all is forgiven. All flushed down the drain.

If I could hold her hand in mine one last time and explain from the start, I'd be forgiven. She cannot hate me forever. She will not hate me forever. Patricia. Patricia? You're out here somewhere, right? Answer my prayers, sweet honey-bun.

If I could stick my cock in her one last time and explain from the start, I'd be forgiven. She cannot hate me forever. She will not hate me forever. Look at the source of my love. The root cause. Hold it next to you, next to yours, your sweet honey-bun.

The resurrection of the dead. Ah, yes, that one. Keep us wondering. A party trick upped a thousand fold. Now you see it, now you don't. Pay no attention to the man behind the curtain.

I'd follow her down any road. Over any rainbow. All that shit. I just need a scent to go on, a mere whiff. A clue. Give me a grid of regional roads, a bottle, a prayer and I'll be there with fuckn bells on.

Patricia, come to me. Come into my lair; hold my brittle spirit in your meaty hands one last time. I didn't do it, Lord, Father, mother, Reverend, sisters, brothers. It was just a cheap party trick, a sleight of hand. The visible and the invisible. To resurrect something dead.

The life of the age to come. Not sure about that. Back in hospital they kept telling me about my life yet to come. About the day I'd be outside again, set free, assuming my position in this world of theirs. Their creation, not His. They made it sound so important. Heavy shit. The drugs had me believing for a while. Clear as fuckn mud.

I want to get down on my knees and worship at her feet, worship her feet alone. She, false idol; me, idolatrous sinner, as unclean as the oil in my 17-year-old car.

Here, in Marmora, up from my knees I walk to the bridge. Stand over the babbling brook. Water runs south toward Lake Ontario. I strip down, bare my ass, bare my soul. A honk. Turn to see a minivan's mother shame-shame me, berating me from behind a pane of tinted glass, the sun brilliant like a halo behind her, kids' innocent faces lit up with glee: something to tell the children of Marmora, the naked madman by the side of the road.

Just a dip. A baptism in the cold, churning water of the Crowe River. The remission of sins. Remember? Wash it away. The memories. Patricia. Paddy. Paddy-cake. Paddy wagon.

I drink, toss the bottle at my car. Spill whisky, the blood of Christ—every drop. Throw my body into the frigid waters, rise again, raise my hands to the sky and call her name, his name: Father, Jesus Christ, all the saints and sinners I can summon, dredged from my memory.

I will not go back to that hospital. I am clean again, again clean.

» » »

The Centre

RICKY & MAY

"So, why's he got custody again? What aren't you tellin' me? You said something afore about a knife, that's all. You just said—'there was a knife'. That don't tell me fuck all. There's knives every fuckn place. Look, here's one."

Ricky holds a butter knife. May looks up from her bowl of soup.

"That ain't a knife. That's fer, like, buttering toast an' shit."

She goes back to her soup.

Ricky snaps back, "Yeah but it's just like your story, see. It just sits there and it don't tell me nothing, don't tell me fuck all."

He starts like he's talking to the butter knife. He holds it up to his face and has a conversation with it, his nose a couple centimetres from the tarnished stainless steel. Ricky looks as crazy as he likely is for a few seconds, then turns his attention back to May.

"I just wanna get the facts in my head the right ways up so's I can make fuckn sense of it. That's all, babe." He goes to put his arm around May but he still has the butter knife in one hand. She shoves him away, picks up her soup bowl and drinks what's left. Some of it dribbles down her chin. She's missing some teeth.

I'm sitting across from her, sitting with this new guy named Harold. I'm telling Harold about the services the Centre offers, what the rules are. Harold's timid and I'm worried some of the others will eat him alive. He's even afraid of me and I work here. Sitting beside me, he sort of cowers, nodding his head to what I say, his arms wrapped around his soup bowl. He's protective of his crackers, his space. But if you said "boo" to him, he'd bolt like a cockroach.

So while I'm here with Harold, I'm also listening to Ricky and May, two regulars. They're a couple, a strange mix, or at least that's what I used to think when I first started working here. Now, nothing seems strange. Ricky's about thirty. May has to be late forties, though her hard living has added ten years to her appearance. Ricky's a chubby white guy. He always wears a Tiger-Cats toque, even when it's thirty-five degrees in August. May's native, likely from Six Nations. Her last name is Hill and I've heard her mention Oshweken a few times. But she's not fresh off the reserve. She's been in the city for a while, knows her way around.

Ricky's on her again, wants to know more about May's kids. "You said three kids, right May? 'Cause I was just like thinking, if we were ever to get us a place together like we talked, then maybe you could, like, get your kids back and they could come live at our place and we could be, like, a family."

May drinks black coffee. Harold nibbles crackers. I should go back to the kitchen to start on the dishes. Some of the clients have returned their trays. But I want to see how it turns out with Ricky and May. I might have to intervene if May starts hollering, like she's done before. She has a temper. It takes her a while but if she's pushed she'll eventually explode. She threw a tray like a Frisbee at another client once, a woman I haven't seen since. May hollered, "Keep your fuckn grubby paws off my old man, you dirty cunt!" And chucked an empty serving tray at this other girl. It bounced off her forehead, cut her open. She went down like a bus hit her. One of the social workers—Linda—drove the woman to hospital. I heard later she got twelve stitches and a tetanus shot. May was shown the door. She was barred from the Centre for a week. Ricky looked smug at the time, seemed to like all the attention. He came in for a few nights bragging about it, strutting around. When May showed up a week later all the bluster went out of him.

Now, Ricky's on her again. "I've always wanted a family, see, May. This one time I sorta got a girl fuckn pregnant, right, but she lost the baby. I've been fuckn busted up about it ever since. That was ten years ago at least. So like, now, your kids could be, like, my kids, I mean it; I really fuckn mean it."

Ricky looks like he's about to cry. He's not normally this soft. I don't know what's come over him. Even Harold looks embarrassed for Ricky. May looks like her blood's slowly boiling as she finishes her coffee. I'm about to step in, to try and change the subject when Harold says something.

"I don't think the lady wants to listen to your shit, brother."

What the hell? Where did that come from? I can't believe it. Harold seems so quiet, so anxious and then he comes out with that. Ricky can't believe it either. He looks around the rest of the table to be sure no one else said it. May looks over at Harold and sort of snickers. Her tension is gone. What Harold said was so out of left field; May just can't be pissed at Ricky any more. Now Ricky's the one who's pissed. He glares at Harold and edges forward on the wooden bench he's on across from me and Harold.

"The fuck you say?"

I decide to give it a minute, to see where it goes, see if they just have a stand-off. Then I hear this clattering noise, like at a wedding. Harold's soup spoon vibrates in his left hand, clanging off the bowl. I check him out and he looks like he's about to piss himself. But then he stands. The clattering noise stops and conversation throughout the Centre stops too. Fuck sakes. Harold must be almost seven feet tall. It was impossible to tell, sitting beside him. His legs must have been stretched out under the table. And not just tall—he's a big fucker, broad shoulders, barrel-chested. But his hands still quake and Ricky sees it. He's not put off by Harold's size. He lunges across the table with the butter knife in his hand. Soup bowls and coffee cups get knocked all around. Harold just stands there like one of those statues on Easter Island. Ricky tries to stick him with the butter knife but it sort of veers off Harold's chest. Ricky crashes to the ground beside the giant man and I land on top of him, grabbing at the blunted shank. Then Harold really starts trembling. He blurts, "I was just standing up for the lady! I was just standing up for the lady!"

Two male social workers and Steve from the kitchen staff come running over. Steve helps me get Ricky to a sitting position on the bench. He drops the butter knife and looks at May. I've got hold of one of his arms; Steve's got the other. Usually stone-faced, May bursts into a wide smile. She leans over the table, taking Ricky's face in both her grubby hands. "My hero," she says and kisses him, open-mouthed, tongues gnashing. I'm only about fifteen centimetres from their mouths and can smell their fetid breath intermingling.

Then May pulls away, still beaming, and says, "I ain't too old yet, Ricky. You know, to have more kids. I might be a grandma but I can fuck with the best of them."

Ricky starts blubbering. I shake my head. It's a Hallmark moment to be sure.

Jenny

Jenny likes to flirt. It gets her things, little extras. When she's had a good day, when she's in a good mood, she'll come to the kitchen counter and really turn it on for me. She smiles wide, darts her brown eyes this way and that. She leans over the counter top, jamming her big breasts up against the glass partition that covers the pots of soup. Her tits mash and expand against the glass and I just can't take my eyes way; it's a truly remarkable sight. She's a bit on the big side but that's what I like. I give her whatever she asks for—extra bread, crackers, a promise of extra pancakes in the morning slathered in syrup; I'd give her my left arm, if she asked. She hams it up, taking whatever I give and walks away shaking her ass. I stand with a ladle in my hand looking like a drooling idiot.

A good day for Jenny is turning a few tricks for quick cash to get booze or drugs; johns that don't blacken her eyes or bust her wrist. I've seen her bad days, when all the spunk is knocked right out of her. At the soup counter, she doesn't look up on nights like that. She lets her long black hair cover her face. She turns up the collar on whatever coat she wears buttoned up tight to cover her breasts and the cigarette burns that scar her skin.

She had nothing but bad days a couple months ago. She's not really a hooker, she just hooks now and again to make ends meet. It depends on who she runs around with. Her trouble started when she paired up with a guy named Bryce who was new to the Centre. No one seemed to know where he came from. He just blew in and blew out and fucked Jenny over in the process. She did no flirting for about three months solid. Some nights she didn't show at all. She'd go three, four nights and then she'd come in, looking worse off than the time before.

The social workers tried to counsel her, but Bryce was always there, hovering over her like he owned her. If Jenny wasn't willing to go with the counsellors for a chat without him, the counsellors could do nothing. I was equally helpless. I tried to make small talk with her while serving soup but she did little more than grunt at me. Bryce, on the other hand, was all smiles, turned on the charm like he had no part in Jenny's misery. He'd yak away with me, Jenny standing in front of him, slouched and bedraggled, dying a slow death.

But what normally happens happened and that was the end of Bryce. There was a confrontation. Somebody kicked the shit out of Bryce. The cops showed one night at the Centre asking about him. A neighbour called in a disturbance right outside the Centre. Bryce was found unconscious, skull fractured, arm broken, ribs smashed, bleeding by the entrance to the alley across the street from the Centre. Someone had even pissed on him. The cops came into the Centre and went round the room, interviewing the clients and the staff. It didn't get them much.

When the cops left, for days after there was chatter about Bryce. Some said he deserved it. Some said he was getting better in hospital, plotting to come back and bust up whoever took him out. Some said I had something to do with it. But that's not on. In my job, I'm obligated to treat all the clients with care and compassion, even if I only run the kitchen, doling out soup after midnight and breakfast at seven in the morning.

Jenny eventually shows. I come back into the Centre at four o'clock in the morning after a walk and she's at the kitchen counter. All the other clients are asleep on the floor and on the wooden benches by the tables. The other kitchen staff and the social workers are playing cards in the supervisor's office. It's the dead of night, a lull that stretches till about five when I start breakfast prep.

I walk into the kitchen, hang up my coat and turn to the counter. Jenny leans over the glass, like she used to, her tits just about bursting through. Her head is down, her long black hair draped across her shoulders, some of it on the glass. Her hands are folded above her head. It looks for a second like she's sleeping standing up. But she's awake. Just a little out of it. I step over and check out her hands. There are cuts and deep ridges full of dirt all over her hands. Her fingers are swollen; weathered and beaten like a fisherman's, like a street whore's. I look around to make sure no one is watching and then reach out and take her hand and kiss it, like she's a princess. This brings her to life. Jenny raises her head off the glass partition and looks at me with weepy eyes.

"Come around, into the kitchen."

I could get fired for bringing a client back here but I don't care.

She comes round into the kitchen. Without the glass between us, Jenny looks shorter.

"What'dya want?" she asks.

"Come on. Back here. Where it's harder to see us."

I lead her over by the walk-in freezer. We sit on a couple of overturned milk crates. It's cold and she starts shivering. I take off my plaid work-shirt and put it over her shoulders. She smiles faintly.

"So, how yah doin'?"

"Better," she says.

"Yeah, you look better. You hungry? You want something?"

"Nah. I can wait till breakfast like the rest of us. Just can't sleep." She fidgets.

I inch forward. I smell her sickly sweet perfume on top of her body odour. Her face is heavily made-up, with mascara blotted in chunks at the corners of her eyes. There's a bit of a bruise on her left cheek that blurs with her make-up. She looks rough but sits lady-like, knees pressed together. It's like we're on a first date in high school.

I don't know what to say. We've never really had a conversation. Just short, funny, flirtatious exchanges over the soup containers. But, then, fuck it, I think. Here she is, within arm's reach, wrapped up in my shirt, looking wounded and lost. And she let me kiss her hand.

I look at her breasts, her black hair, her dirty fingernails. I lean forward to kiss her. Jenny doesn't react. She just sits there and waits for it. I kiss her. Her lips are dry, rough—they don't move. It's almost like she doesn't know how to kiss. I pull back and she's expressionless, blank.

And then there's a bang on the kitchen counter behind us. Me and Jenny both turn. A big, gristly dude with his head wrapped in a red bandana barks, "Jenny, get your ass back on this side where it belongs."

Without looking at me, she stands slowly and does like she is told.

The guy glares at me. "Don'tcha got some fuckn work to do, asshole?"

I don't answer. I've never seen him before. Another

Centre newcomer. I turn my face away and stare at my running shoes.

Lucy, Stacey & Stan

A bit of an odd couple, Lucy and Stan but—as mentioned—that's nothing new. Stacey is Lucy's daughter and she hates Stan. I have no idea who her real dad is. But I have a soft spot for her, for any of the kids who come into the Centre. Usually it's single moms with dirty toddlers or foul-mouthed youngsters copping serious attitude. They never make eye contact at the soup counter. Too cool, too hard, for that.

"Chicken vegetable or tomato pasta?" I ask politely.

"Don't care. Whatever. You fuckn choose."

That's followed by a slap to the back of the head from their mom.

Stacey is older, early teens. She's embarrassed to come to the Centre but realizes it's necessary for her survival. Stan's a prick. Big, red drunk's nose lined with busted capillaries and he's rude and belligerent to Lucy. She just takes it, rolls with it; rolls with whatever it takes to have a man by her side. Lucy's a tragic case—but aren't they all.

I've had words with Stan before. I don't like the way he talks to Lucy and Stacey. In the soup line, he'll snap at them, order them around, insult both of them loudly. I tell him to knock it off. Lucy always shrugs. Stacey scowls or looks embarrassed, eager to take her food and find a dark corner to hide in.

They're not here every night. Technically—I've learned—they're not homeless. Lucy uses a fixed address; at her sister's somewhere near Sanford Avenue. So when they get their cheques they're not around the first ten days of the month or so. But they eventually return. And maybe just Lucy and Stan at first. Stacey holds off, is tolerated by her aunt and actually goes to school for the first couple weeks of the month. When Lucy and Stan come in, it's a night here and there at first but by the last week of the month, all three of them are here every night. The deeper into the month it gets, the more Stan shows up pissed, the more Lucy looks battered and wounded, the more Stacey looks terrified, looks like she wants to run from it all. It's a predictable, ugly cycle that plays itself out each month.

But I'll say this for Stan: he watches out for both mother and daughter in his own macho way. Because there's no shortage of predators in the Centre and on the streets, predators who would love to take Stacey and corrupt her fully beyond repair. A few times he's come to her defence, confronted guys like Bryce or the bandana boy Jenny hangs with, and kept them away from Stacey. Stacey seems sort of ambivalent about it. She hates Stan for how he treats her mom but there's also visible little-girl fear on her face when some older guy comes sniffing around.

Tonight Stacey is particularly withdrawn. I try to coax a smile out of her when she gets her soup and sandwich but she offers nothing, just takes her tray and shuffles over to a bench and a table to eat the same shitty food she did last night. It's February 28th. If it's any consolation, it's the shortest month of the year and welfare cheques seem to come quicker. But Stacey looks beyond consolation. From the kitchen I watch her nibble her sandwich, take tiny sips of her soup. Then Stan and Lucy come over.

"Chicken noodle or cream of mushroom?"

"Mushroom," Lucy says.

"Sandwich?"

"Guess so."

She barely looks up as she skulks away with her tray.

Then Stan's in front of me. I'm about to curtly ask him what he wants to eat when he leans over the counter, elbows up, his face kind of tucked down in his chest. I ease back a bit, not sure what he's up to, plus he reeks of booze.

"What's up, Stan?"

"Listen, keep it quiet for a sec, alright? I need a favour."

"From me?"

He shifts uncomfortably. Looks me straight in the eye "Yeah, that's right. I know you got no use for me but this is for Stacey I'm askin'. So I'm hopin' you can do somethin', somethin' special 'cause tomorrow is her sixteenth birthday." He pauses for a second. "Well, not really tomorrow.

She was born in a leap year, on February 29th for fuck sakes. It's s'posed to bring her luck but just look at her; you see any fuckn luck over there?" He nudges his chin over his shoulder toward Lucy and Stacey. There's no one else in line for soup, so I let him carry on, plus this is a departure for him.

"I can't do fuckn nothin' for her till next week when I get my cheque. I promised her a new pair of winter boots. She wants one of them furry kind the kids are all wearing again. She's gone all winter in a pair of rain boots; her feet freeze every night when we walk over here. She's a good kid most of the time but this ain't no fuckn place to celebrate your sixteenth birthday." Stan looks sad for a second. Then starts again. "I remember my sixteenth birthday. My old man paid for a whore to make me a fuckn man. Then she did him too. Two-for-one birthday special or somethin'. We were both pissed drunk. It was about the only good night I ever had with the old prick. Course I don't want nothin' fuckn like that for Stacey. You've seen the fuckers round here, lookin' to get a piece."

Stan's voice trails off so I cut in. "Then what'd'ya have in mind?"

"A cake. At breakfast when she wakes up. Just a cake. You work in a fuckn kitchen, you can bake a cake, right? It's Lucy's idea, to tell the truth. But I'm doin' the askin'."

This is out of character for him and it's hard to resist a show of heart from the sloshed old prick.

"I can do that."

"Good. And thanks." Then Stan grabs a sandwich and walks away, over to Lucy and Stacey.

At seven o'clock, it's the first thing I do. I come out from behind the counter with the cake in my hands. I even found some candles, though only six—it's close enough.

Lucy and Stan are awake. Stacey is still asleep on the floor, her head wedged under a bench, using her jacket for a pillow. Lucy goes over and wakes her. I put the cake down on the table and step back quickly, respecting their privacy. But as usual, as she comes to, Stacey looks embarrassed. She tries her best not to smile but can't pull it off. Lucy hugs her. Stan kisses her on the cheek. Then from the back of the room, someone starts signing "Happy Birthday." By the time they get to the end of the song, half the clients and staff in the room have joined in. There is applause. A few assholes complain about the noise, the delay in breakfast. Stan snaps at them and that's the end of that. Lucy cuts a piece of cake and passes it to her daughter on her sweet sixteenth. Stacey smiles fully. I go back to the kitchen, leaving them to it.

» » »

One Night in Oktober

Phelps is so drunk he thinks he can speak German. He sings what he thinks are the lyrics: "Ziggy, ziggy, ziggy, OY! OY! OY!"

The arena floor is soaked in beer and sweat. Phelps is so drunk he thinks he can polka. A woman named Sofia hangs off his arm. Her haired is coloured jet-black. Phelps holds her up or she holds him up. It's hard to tell. She wears a brilliant red sweater with the neck cut low. She has beautiful breasts. In the middle of the polka, Phelps has been leaning into her and staring down her sweater at her wonderful, deep cleavage. She knows it and could care less.

The chanting stops and the accordions zoom into a new song. Phelps twirls Sofia around. She pirouettes in the beer and then he pulls her in close. They mash together. Phelps frantically nods his head to the music, puts one arm around her waist, raises her other hand high and they quasi-polka again. They lurch and list, his face in her tits. They bounce off couples but no one cares. Everyone is so smashed that any imposition is tolerated. They pick up the pace, bouncing and jostling, sloshing in spilled beer. Then Phelps leans in too close. He smells Sofia's sweat and perfume. But when he leans back out, he jolts his head up and slams the crown of his head into Sofia's face. She tears her hands away from him. They stand looking at each other in the centre of the dance floor. The Oktoberfest music blares on. Sofia starts to bleed. It gushes dark red from her nose.

"Fuck, sorry."

Sofia can't hear him. She jams one hand to her face and then grabs his left hand, pulling Phelps off the dance floor. He brings her face in close and examines her nose. It's not broken, just badly bloodied. But it looks terrible. Sofia doesn't seem to mind.

"Fuck, sorry."

She brings Phelps close and kisses him for the first time. He tastes blood and sweat.

People stare. A woman comes over.

"You okay, dear?" she hollers.

She wears one of those green felt Oktoberfest hats. She looks more Robin Hood than German. Phelps is embarrassed and worried. But Sofia steps right up.

"I'm good, thanks. Just this fucker's way of picking me up." She points a thumb at Phelps. They're frozen for a second, waiting for the humour to hit. Sofia laughs. The woman titters nervously and then slinks away. Then Sofia kisses Phelps again. It's great but he's a little uneasy still, wary of onlookers. He pulls away a couple seconds later. He wants the bleeding to stop. He wipes his mouth with the back of his hand. Then his hand on his shirt. Phelps pinches her nose and tries to staunch the bleeding. He leads her to the washrooms.

Sofia comes out five minutes later all cleaned up, smiling and no longer bleeding. She's good as new.

"Fuck, sorry."

"You say anything else?"

"Yeah, you wanna dance some more?"

"Nah. Enough for me. Let's leave."

Phelps grabs his coat from the back of a chair. His friends have scattered. They won't miss him.

Phelps and Sofia grab a taxi. He kisses her in the backseat. Then she presses his face down into her chest. Phelps sort of suckles there, breathing her in.

Back at her place, Sofia gets a couple beers.

"Your shirt," she says.

Her blood is all over the front.

"I'm surprised the cabbie gave us a ride."

"He's seen worse. They make a killing this time of year in this town. They're prepared for barf and blood in October."

"Yeah, s'pose so."

Then Sofia takes off her red sweater, just like that. She stands in the centre of her living room in a black bra and black jeans. Phelps gets up off the sofa and goes to her.

"Not so fast, follow me."

She leads him into her bedroom and takes off her jeans and panties. She pulls off his bloodied shirt, works his pants open. She gets down and sucks his cock. Phelps looks at her black hair across her back, the black bra just visible. Then they're on the bed. She pulls Phelps on top of her and bites his lip hard. He bleeds, which seems fair. Phelps starts fumbling with her cunt but she's not having it. She pushes his hand away. They fuck for a while next but she decides she doesn't want that either. Sofia grabs his cock and jerks him off. Phelps wants her to stop but he looks at her black hair, the black bra and he comes on her stomach. She looks up at Phelps and smears some come on her fingers. Then she puts one hand on his ass and starts pulling his ass cheeks apart. She tries to rub his come on his ass and with her right index finger she tries to finger his asshole. Phelps squirms away. He's drunk enough to polka but not drunk enough to have his own come up his arse. Sofia laughs and takes her hand away and puts it near his face. Phelps looks at her incredulously. He's not licking that.

"Just smell," she says.

Phelps makes like he does. Then she reaches behind him and drags her fingernails down his back, hard, breaking the skin, drawing more blood. It hurts like hell but what can he do. She's determined. Maybe even angry or vengeful.

Sofia pushes Phelps off. She reaches down and jerks herself off. Phelps just lies there watching, sort of, the bed spinning wildly. When she's done she starts jerking him off again but it doesn't go anywhere. Phelps puts his face in her smoky, black hair and falls asleep.

In the morning Sofia stands in a kimono beside the bed. The room stinks of sweat and beer. Phelps tries to lie perfectly still, to keep the hangover at bay. Sofia drinks coffee.

"I washed your shirt. Got most of the blood out."

"Uh-huh. Thanks."

She sits down beside him. She starts jerking Phelps off but his cock is pretty sore. Phelps pulls away and she gets it. Sofia takes a big drink of coffee and holds it in her mouth. She swallows, leans over and sucks Phelps off. Her mouth is warm, almost hot. Phelps comes quickly. She sits back up and finishes her coffee.

"You gotta write something before you leave."

Phelps look around. The walls of her bedroom are

scrawled on: words, crude drawings, some of them dated, names signed. He didn't notice it in the dark last night.

"Oh yeah?"

"Yeah, write whatever you want."

She hands Phelps a thick black magic marker.

"I'm going for a shower. Your clothes are over there on the chair."

Phelps reads some of the stuff on her walls. Sentimental, stupid rhymes mostly. One drawing that's not bad. Sofia must get a lot of visitors. It sickens him for a second or maybe it's the hangover.

Phelps finds a spot on the wall by the foot of the bed and writes, "Sofia, you make red the world's truest colour." She'll wonder whether he means the sweater or her bloody nose. It's his attempt at being poetic, clever. Or maybe she won't even read it, won't think anything or just think that Phelps is an asshole.

He gets up and puts on his clothes and goes out to the living room. Sofia comes out of the bathroom. She's in the kimono still but her hair is wet. She brushes it. She doesn't say anything. Phelps takes the hint and goes over and puts on his shoes. They reek of beer.

At the door, Sofia pulls him close and bites his lip again but not hard enough to bleed. Still, his eyes water like he's been punched.

"Come back another time if you want."

She sounds like Mae West. Her kimono is open at the

front. Phelps is tempted to dive into her cleavage but thinks better of it. He click-clacks down the stairs in his stinky beer shoes away from her second storey apartment.

Phelps walks a few blocks and tries to get his bearings. He has to meet up with his friend who lives in Kitchener. He was supposed to sleep at his place last night.

On King Street Phelps finds a taxi and gets in. The driver has about six air freshener trees dangling.

"Where to?"

Phelps has his friend's address scrawled on a piece of paper in his wallet. He pulls it out. "257 Weber." But he pronounces it the German way: "Vehber," trying to impress the driver. The driver could care less. He looks like he's from the Middle East.

As the cabbie pulls away from the curb, Phelps lets his head loll to the left, out of the glare of the morning sun. The scratches on his back sting, even leaning against the soft, deeply-impressed seat in the cab. The scratches will take a while to heal and likely leave scars. Phelps deserves it for nearly breaking Sofia's nose. Then he thinks of the writing on her bedroom wall. There must have been thirty different messages, thirty different men. Phelps shifts in his seat and begins to worry.

» » »

Everybody Loses

The cook and the waitress are making plans for lottery winnings.

The cook goes, "I'd pay off the house. Buy a better vehicle. Take a trip someplace warm with Steve. Quit this job in a fuckn flash and go back to school at the college down Bellville. Accounting or computers or both. Not sure. Nancy's sister done something down there. I just wanna do it. 'Cause sure as fuck I'd never work no more."

The waitress fires back, "Me, I'd move someplace warm. Down Florida. Buy a big house on the water. Guess Frank can come. Though he'd havtah be a lot fuckn nicer to me it comes to that." She looks like she means it for a second and then they both laugh. "New truck. Speedboat. Fix Tiffany's teeth. PlayStation shit galore for Cameron.

And I'd get my tits done. Swear I would. Havtah, living on the beach year round. And yeah, fuck this job in no time flat. They're gonna need to get them two new staff right quick, eh?"

They both laugh some more and then turn away from each other to their work. The cook stands over the deep fryer. The waitress stares down at her pad of scrawled orders as she walks to the cash register.

It's the third week of April and grey snow covers eastern Ontario. Snow after Easter. Right when you think winter is done it comes back and kicks you once more. It happens every year but still people act surprised, pissed about it. The women have it right, dreaming of sun and sand.

I'm sitting at the table nearest the kitchen sipping bad coffee, waiting on a lunch order. It's nearly three o'clock and well past the lunch rush, if they have one in Norwood. Sylvia, my wife, has gone across the street to a place called Clement's Variety with our daughter Alexandra to get her something sweet. "Some junk," Alexandra likes to say. The junk will help keep her quiet in the car. It's a long drive yet.

At the table across from me an old woman scratches lottery tickets. A bowl of soup cools in front of her. One table over from her a man younger than me in paint and drywall-dust stained jeans and work shirt flips through the *Toronto Sun*. A burger sits in front of him. At the table by the window two teenagers who should be in school chew on pizza slices. Above us all, fixed to the wood-panelled walls, battered radio speakers spurt details about the size of the weekly jackpot, Junior B hockey play-off scores and an announcement about an outdoor bake sale supposed to be this weekend in Hastings that will be cancelled because of the snow. Outside the restaurant's window on Highway 7 a transport rumbles by. It gears up after passing the only stoplight in town.

I hear the sizzle of chips in grease. I look back behind the counter at the cook and the waitress.

The cook goes, "Course what are the odds, eh?"

The waitress, with her right index finger punching keys on the cash register, calls back over her shoulder, "Yeah but someone's gotta win, right. Might as well be you or me."

The cook holds up chips in a wire basket under a cloud of greasy steam. "Not necessarily, Marilyn. Sometimes it might take weeks, right?"

The waitress thinks about it a moment. Then says, "Yeah, they fuckn set it up that ways somehow. Keep stringing people along. Keep us hanging on."

I want to join the conversation. The waitress—Marilyn—has nailed it. Someone somewhere always strings us along, keeps us hanging on. But I'm an interloper, so I say nothing. My vehicle—as they say round here—is a giveaway for starters. Instead of a truck or Rez car I drive a small, fuel-efficient import. I'm from out of town but that's not that strange in a roadside highway restaurant. Still, round here, folks are used to locals, to truckers, to OPP cops, not city folk trying to avoid 401 chaos.

I keep my opinions to myself. I fill my mouth with coffee instead. I look out the window again. I stretch my neck and look for Sylvia and Alexandra.

A minute later the old woman—her spoilt, losing lottery tickets discarded next to an ashtray—heads off in the direction of the washrooms. The guy in workman's clothes tosses his newspaper on a chair. Then he scoops up his burger. The kids by the window wash down their pizza slices with Coke. Beyond them traffic kicks up slush.

Then the cook calls out that my order's done. The waitress retrieves it and brings it over. She puts my fish and chips, Sylvia's Caesar salad and Alexandra's chicken bits and chips on the table in front of me.

"You gonna eat all that, hon?"

I meet her eyes. "Wife and kid just ran across the street for something. They'll be back in a second."

"I know. Seen them cross the road. Just teasing. I'll bring their drinks when theys get back."

She starts to walk toward the kids at the front window as she says it. She doesn't give me a chance to reply. I catch a whiff of her in her wake: sickly sweet perfume mingled with kitchen grease. I can't help but look at her ass for a second. The outline of her underwear is visible through her white server's trousers. When I take my eyes away, the paint and drywall guy is looking at me. He busts me on behalf of the waitress who is, for all I know, his wife, his sister, his cousin. I feel like a prick and reach for the salt.

Seconds later, I hear the squeal of tires and the crunch of metal. There's a faint, muffled scream from the road. The waitress shrieks by the front of the restaurant and calls out to the cook, "Jesus, Pat! Come quick!" The cook comes running from the kitchen, wiping her hands on her apron. The kids at the window bolt from their seats. One of them knocks over a Coke. A brown smear spreads on the linoleum. The worker turns slowly to regard the road. The old woman with the losing lottery tickets has not returned from the shitter.

It takes me longer to realize what's happened. I'm too busy working on my first mouthful of chips. And maybe because I'm not from here. Maybe because my head is still fuzzy from the numbing effects of the drive. Maybe because I'm too concerned about how much salt will liven my dreary lunch. But then it hits me.

I stand but don't move to the front window. The waitress and cook hug. Then the waitress turns and looks at me. Her eyes search mine. Outside, the two pizza and pop kids slide around on the snowy sidewalk. The burger guy has turned away from the window to look at me too. There is still no sign of the old woman.

I go up on my tip-toes. Through a mess of crunched

pickup truck and Pontiac, I see Sylvia on the other side of the highway. Both her hands are cupped over her mouth, stifling a scream. Her eyes are wide—wider than I've ever seen before—centred on something a couple metres in front of her. She looks likes she's not breathing. She looks like her head will burst—be torn from her body from the pressure of holding in her scream—and rocket into the grey clouds above.

It hits me in the knees first, then the gut. I feel like I'm going to vomit. Then a second before I retch, Sylvia's hands come away from her mouth and her arms spread wide. Alexandra appears from nowhere. She jumps into Sylvia's arms. I see Sylvia squeeze Alexandra's small body with the strength of a thousand men. I finish chewing my chips and swallow hard. I taste bile with my lunch. All talk of sun and sand is forgotten.

» » »

Smooth with the Ladies

9:54 P.M.

As Chester Alburn drunkenly belts out his best Hank Williams, Darren Druce slides his left hand up Marcie Dembrowski's thigh—Chester's woman, or so Chester thinks. It's karaoke night at the Havelock Hotel. Darren and Henry Stinson came down from Warsaw by snow-machine. Thirty kilometres or so, just to get juiced. To laugh their arses off at the knobs trying to sing, trying to be rock stars, trying to impress their women. Friday night. Darren and Henry are out to have a good one. Paid yesterday. Wallets fat with cash. Monday morning a long way off.

Middle of February, colder than a witch's nip, and Marcie's wearing a skirt. She's got enough sense to wear thick, black tights underneath. Darren's callused hand catches on the material right when the song ends, fingers inching closer to her snatch, other hand wrapped around a bottle of Molson Canadian. Marcie jerks back, smiles wickedly at Darren, starts clapping like Chester's old Hank #1 himself. Darren appreciates her enthusiasm and Chester's balls, if not his singing. He puts his thumb over the end of his bottle and clonks it against the table. Puts his smoke to his lips and sharply inhales, hoping to catch a whiff of Marcie on his fingers. No such luck. Song was too damned short.

Henry stands. "Nuther?"

Darren regards him crookedly. "Dumb fuckn question is that?"

"Just being polite."

"Well don't."

Henry slumps to the bar. Darren was just about there with Marcie and now he's dejected, pissed. He could do without Henry's obvious question, his dumber than dumb monotone voice. Henry's a bit slow. Not nearly as smooth with the ladies as Darren, or so Darren thinks.

Chester plops down in his chair and slides an arm around Marcie, drawing her in close, kissing her on the cheek. Marcie stares at Darren the whole time. Eyes like daggers cut him to the quick.

Henry's back with beers. Darren grabs his and waves it at an empty table.

"Seat over there opened up."

"Thought we was talkin' with Marcie."

"No. Done with that now, Henry. Fuckn get it?"

Henry looks unsure.

Marcie cuts in, "Have yerselves a good time fellahs."

"Count on it."

Chester kicks back in his chair, slaps Marcie's right thigh. "Where you boys fuckn off to? We was just gettin' ta know each other. Yous tellin' me about that operation yous into up Centre Dummer."

Darren swigs beer. Looks at Marcie. He wants no more of either of them. "I was talkin' shit. There's a reason that place called Centre Dummer. Full of dumb fucks don't know their ass from a hole in the ground."

"That a fact?" Chester says.

Marcie smiles wide.

Then Chester goes, "The Missus here from South Dummer. What's that mean you sayin' 'bout her?"

Marcie goes googly-eyed. Chester snorts. Then carries on, "Fact is, Marcie knows perfectly well her ass from a hole in the ground." He spits beer as he says it. Laughs. Tries to pull himself together, manages, "Show him, dear."

Marcie stands, shows Darren her back and shakes her black-skirted mud-flaps. Chester reaches round and rubs her ass cheeks, winks at Darren. But he can't contain himself. Puts his head on the table and roars with laughter. Best time he's had in ages. Marcie sits and Chester pops up his head. Regains his composure. Porn-kisses her in front of the lads—exaggerated tongue, one hand on her tit. When he's done, "On your way fellahs. Run along and play. Don't bring your shit round here no more."

10:40 P.M.

Dolly Ferguson and Missy Munro cackle into drinks. A couple old maids, other side of fifty; first started coming to the Havelock Hotel when the Ladies and Escorts entrance was still in use. Unmarried—both of them—all these years.

Dolly owns a little place out Chase Corners. Missy lives in town. Nights she's too tired—forget about too pissed, never even a consideration—to drive the truck back to Chase Corners, Dolly crashes on Missy's sofa; it's led to a bit of speculation. No husbands. Out cougaring around. Empty-handed when the bar closes, probably take matters into their own hands.

Other day, standing outside the Havelock Gardens Chinese and Canadian Food Restaurant, Ollie Aquin was rehashing a night at the Hotel with Walter McKinney.

"Bulls they are. Sure of it. Sure as fuckn rain."

"Eh? What you on about? Heads?"

"Not livestock, Walter. Them two I was tellin' you 'bout. Bulls. Dykes. Lezzies. Yah know. Dolly Ferguson up Chase Corners and Missy Munro here in town. Lives by the rink. They get up to it with each other. Sure as I'm standing here."

Walter regards him just so. "Round here? In Havelock?"

"'Fraid so. Everywhere nowadays. Disgustin' you ask me."

Walter toed a discarded packet of soy sauce. "Thought they only did that sorta shit down Terrawna."

"Not no more. Goes on all over . . ."

"Nuther round ladies?" Darren stands when he says it.

Missy leans into Dolly's padded shoulder, giggling. "Should we?" she says in Dolly's ear.

Dolly winks at Darren. Puts a finger up, meaning jut a sec. Turns to face Missy. She whispers, "Guess another won't hurt nobody."

They hold up empty glasses. "If you wouldn't mind, dear," Missy says, all older-woman sweet but sexy.

Darren pads off to the bar.

Henry struggles for words. Looks from Dolly to Missy, the makeup glare on their sallow cheeks muddy in the barroom light.

Dolly takes the initiative. "You wanna step outside, smoke a dube?"

"Eh?"

Missy joins in. "Just nip out for a toke while your friend's at the bar. Won't take but a minute. Get a buzz on. Help us get talkin'. Get to know one another."

Henry looks over to the bar. Darren's crowded at the back of a mob trying to get in orders. Henry scratches his balls under the tabletop. Examines his blackened fingernails.

"Don't know."

"Yah don't smoke?"

More scratches. "Course ah do."

"Can't hurt then, eh?"

"'Spose not. What 'bout Darren? He'll get pissed."

"We can always go back out and smoke another. Just leave your jacket here to save the table."

Outside in the minus-thirty air, Henry sucks a joint. Then stammers, "Cold as f-f-f-fuck."

"Got that right."

Blows smoke, hands over the dube. Through gritted teeth, "Good shit."

Dolly and Missy take quick hits then hand the joint back to Henry.

"Cold is right," Dolly says, shouldering in close to Missy.

Missy goes, "You fellahs not from Havelock, eh? Don't know what they say 'bout us, then?"

Henry sucks the joint. Looks blank. Shakes his head as he exhales. Offers it back, but both women decline. Dolly turns Missy's face, leans in, kisses her hard. Missy returns it. Henry stands stock-still, then shivers, bug-eyed. The women mash together. Sweatered breasts smeared against sweatered breasts. A hand each on the other's ass. Tongues out. Eyes closed. Grunts. Moans. Having their Friday night fun.

Henry takes one last hit from the joint then pitches it into the snow before bolting inside.

Five minutes later, Darren returns, expensive drinks in hand. "Here we go ladies. Drink up. Down the hatch. Get 'em in yah! We're gonna party tonight!"

Henry coughs. Watches Dolly and Missy take their gin and tonics. Summer drink in the middle of February. Thinks: fuck's up with these two anyway? Turns to Darren. Says behind a hand, "Don't think this gonna work out good."

"What?"

"These two," he starts, then stops.

"Fuck off and drink, Henry. Do yourself a favour. Don't think, don't speak." Darren stabs a finger at Henry's beer bottle. "Just drink, gearbox."

Henry goes to say something, then stops. Sucks on his brown pop instead. Darren does likewise, stupid grin on his face behind the bottle. Dolly and Missy suck back G & Ts. Only sucking there'll be among them.

12:04 A.M.

Liquored but still unlucky, Darren watches a woman alone at a table. No jackets on other chair backs. After a while, he goes over. Throws a leg over a chair, sits. Henry does likewise, a pace or two behind.

"Well, well," Darren starts. "Ain't seen you afore. New round here?"

The woman leans forward, elbows propped on the table, grey cardigan sweater frayed, hair pulled back into a long, salt and pepper ponytail. She peers over tinted glasses, chin just above her white wine. Cheeks flushed scarlet.

"Live outside town a bit. I'm new to the area. Both me and my husband are."

She says it and pauses, naively thinking it's enough to chase away Darren and Henry.

"I came to the tavern to meet some local people. Get to know some of you. Maybe promote my work."

Darren and Henry glance at each other: what-the-fuck-promote-what? looks on their faces.

The woman reaches into a macramé satchel. Pulls out a business card. Places it on the table next to the ashtray.

"I'm Agnes Dujic. A potter, as it says on the card. Maybe you've read about me in the *Examiner*, heard about my show at the gallery in Peterborough."

Darren and Henry still got what-the-fuck looks going.

Agnes carries on, head glazed in a white wine buzz. "I'd heard there were many artists and artisans out here. Couldn't take the big city hubbub in Peterborough any more. Rudolph and me bought a charming little place out at Rush Point a few months back. The tranquility is good for my work, opens the pores and out comes my creativity."

Darren waits, then says, "What'd yah talking 'bout, potter?"

"Potter. I'm an artist. Make forms with my hands from clay."

She holds up her hands as proof: swollen fingers, chalky skin.

"You mean bowls and shit? Fuck sakes. You make a livin' doing that?"

Agnes smiles.

Darren shakes his head. Then nods at Henry to go for a round of drinks. Leans in close to Agnes, eyes what are—despite the ratty cardigan—super-sized tits.

"So then, where's this Rudy now, Aggie?"

Agnes smiles and points to the gents. "Rudolph should be back any minute."

Darren thinks different. He'd been watching her for a good ten minutes before he sat down. No way her old man could be in the can that long. Unless of course he slipped away somewhere with someone. But who the fuck would go anywhere with someone named Rudolph? Reindeer's stupid fucking name, Darren thinks.

He snickers. "That your story?"

"Story?"

"How many ah them glasses you had tonight, Aggie?"

"Enough."

"Enough to come home with me?"

Smooth with the ladies.

Agnes gulps her wine. Eyes the gents again. "You're very forward."

"Forward is fuckn right."

"What happened to your friend?"

Darren snorts. "What'd yah mean by that, Aggie? You mean me *and* Henry? Fuck sakes, you a team player there old Agnes?" He looks at her tits again, deliberate-like, slurs. "'Cause if so, Henry can have his fun when I'm done with yous."

Agnes bats her eyelashes, unbothered. At least appears so. Checks the washroom. No sign of Rudolph. "Well, that wasn't really what I had in mind," she says, rimming her finger round the lip of her wine glass.

Darren's a bit confused. Still, she's not said no, not told him to fuck off completely. That's always a good sign. More than enough to go on, far as he's concerned. He's practically frothing at the mouth. Pushed up against the table. Eyes wide. Fat cock in his jeans.

"What'd yah mean exactly?"

Agnes downs her wine. "Well, it wouldn't really be fair to Rudolph to miss out on all the fun." She's not making eye contact. Pauses, then goes, "My, my, didn't think we'd get up to this sort of sport so quick out here."

Darren's not really sure any more. Hard-on gone. Eases back in his chair. Eyes narrowed.

"That not the sort of team play you were thinking of?" Agnes asks, eyes now centred on Darren. "When you said team player, I assumed you were up for any type of group action. It's all the rage now, my dear." Agnes folds her potter's hands in front of her on the table, poised. Regards Darren just so.

"Lady . . ." he starts. "I'm not . . . Fuck sakes . . . You're not? . . . You serious?"

"You figure it out, dear. If you're interested, we'll be over at the bar."

She stands slowly as she says it, leans forward, heavy breasts surging toward Darren.

He says nothing. Eyes murky. Wasted. No clear thoughts. Stays firmly rooted where he is. Doesn't budge. Waits for Henry to get back with another round of beers.

1:22 A.M.

Ashley Fargo rises from her knees, blundering out to the street when she hears her brother's voice. "Fuck, that's Marvin," she says over her shoulder.

"Marvin? Who tha fuck's Marvin?" Henry goes. He tugs at his zipper, dick steaming in the frigid air. "Your old man?"

Ashley horks cum and spit into a snowbank, calls back, "Worse, my brother."

Darren leans against the Havelock Gardens Chinese and Canadian Food Restaurant. Ashley's the sort of team player he had in mind. Found her skulking in the corridor near the men's can in the Hotel. Turned over a rock and there she was. Curly black hair. Gobs of gooey mascara. Bad skin, pockmarks. Pink belly shirt in the middle of winter. Low-cut jeans with G-string undies sticking out the back of her too-fat ass. A real small-town dirty. She blew him in the Hotel parking lot, then offered to do Henry by the dumpster behind the restaurant. Two blowjobs for some Chinese takeout. That was just the start. Said Darren and Henry get her a bottle, they could go back to her place and party till dawn. Darren was on it like a shot. Went back and paid the Hotel bartender fifty bucks for an unopened twenty-sixer of CC. Took a couple hits waiting on Henry to get his hummer when some big fucker came over, calling Ashley's name.

Darren shifts the bottle behind his back.

Marvin approaches. "Cold fuckn night to be standin' round."

Darren looks up at him. "Came outside for a butt."

"What, no smokin' no more in tha Chink's?"

"Yeah. New policy. Sumpin' like that."

"Don't get fuckn smart."

Darren looks beyond the big man for Henry. He could use a little help. Then Ashley appears. Marvin's eyes light up. Glares first at Darren, then Ashley.

"Sluttin' around again, Ash?" He says it flatly.

She doesn't get too close. "Maybe. Fuckn business is it of yours?"

"All you get up to's my business."

"That fuckn so?"

"Fuckn right. You knows it. We got ourselves a deal, right?"

Ashley stubs her boot against the restaurant's front step, yellow neon light shining down on her pallid cheeks. Inside, Jake Ming sucks on a smoke, trying to look through the iced-up window at what's going on. Ready to call the cops the first sign of violence—he's replaced his front window three times in the last year. Insurance company plans to raise his premium.

Henry comes out to the street, panting, half-smiling. Dumb fuck, Darren thinks.

"Two of 'em, eh?" Marvin says. "Double my usual cut, then?" He looks down at Ashley. "You went over your rates afore you started this shit, right?"

Ashley's face whitens more. She starts to stammer a response when Marvin turns to Darren. "You fellahs paid up front, right?" His voice not so flat any more.

Bottle clenched in his gloved, right hand, Darren goes, "Fuck you on about?"

Henry sees the bottle. Steps behind Marvin.

Marvin goes, "Ashley works for me. Me and her got a deal, right. Got sick of you fucks takin' it from her all ah time. Decide we might as well make a little coin from her whorin' ways. Get it, fuckface?"

"All she's gettin' is some rice and fuckn chicken balls for her troubles. Ain't paying for a fuckn lousy blowjob," Darren says, then lunges forward, waving the bottle at Marvin's head. But he slides on the ice as he does so, losing purchase on the sidewalk. Bottle flies loose, over Marvin's head, bounces harmlessly off a parked, black pickup into the street. The top cracks off and rye sloshes onto grey snow. Henry goes to jump Marvin's back but he sloughs Henry off as if he were a kid. Ashley takes off down the street. Weaponless, Darren steps forward awkwardly, right into Marvin's left fist. Hits him square on the chin. Goes down fast, head bouncing off the restaurant's concrete steps. Henry knows Darren's knocked out. Watches Ashley scamper away. He looks for the bottle, a slab of solid icicle, something heavy to throw at Marvin. Nothing.

Jake steps outside, intervenes. "Take your shit somewheres else, Marvin."

Marvin glares at him. "Just trying to collect what's mine. Not your affair, Jake."

"It happens outside my shop, it's my fuckn business." Jake looks at Henry cowering next to Darren. "You owe Marvin for sumpin'?"

Henry says nothing. Whimpers a little. Knows he's beat. Tries shaking Darren awake. Not sure what to say without Darren's help. Dumb as a fucking stump. He looks up, sees Marvin coming at him. Jake stands there, spatula in one hand, phone in the other, not ready to help Henry, just ready to call the cops if his restaurant is threatened.

Henry glances at Darren. Reaches over and stuffs his hand in Darren's back pocket. Takes out his wallet. Grabs all the cash—maybe eighty bucks—and throws it at Marvin.

Marvin scoops it. "Wise move, pussy-lips. You come sniffin' around my sister's hole again, you remember this and pay up front next time."

Henry nods, slack-jawed. "What about Darren?" Then looks at Jake.

Marvin goes to Jake, "You should get this shit cleaned up off your doorstep. Fucker's passed out drunk. Could freeze to death. Not good for business, Jake."

Jake hits the cop shop on speed-dial. Marvin jams the bills in his front pocket and looks around for Ashley. She's long gone. Henry seizes his opportunity—races for his snow machine out back the Hotel. So full of booze he can barely stand, he slumps onto the snowmobile. Starts it up quick. Makes tracks by moonlight for Warsaw alone.

» » »

Aquamarine

Billy Arnason packs in his job at Krazy Kevin's TV and Stereo. He just can't take it any more. He's tired of lying to people he sees later on the streets, at the bar and in the arena.

And he's ready to pack it in with Debbie too.

He calls Rooster McMulken. Rooster drives a beer store truck.

"Rooster, meet me in the parking lot behind Kevin's. And drop a case on your way over."

"Gimme twenty minutes."

Billy walks to the back of the store. He pushes open the door into the parking lot and lights up a cigarette. He loosens his tie, undoes the top button on his shirt. He looks up into the sky and breathes freely for the first time all day.

Walters, the sales manager, comes out back.

"You sure about this, Billy? You been with us seven years. Put in some good years."

"You got that right. But, yeah, I'm sure. I can't take the bullshit any longer."

Walters looks at him sideways. "Bullshit. What bullshit?"

"You don't want me to answer that."

"Okay. Your call. But clean out your shit today. Carolyn will send your last cheque and record of employment in the mail." Walters pauses for a second. "You know you're leaving us short. You sure you can't make it for two more weeks?"

"Don't beg me. I'm not worth it. And, besides, my mind's made up."

"Okay, fine. Like I said; your call. Nice working with you, Billy."

Billy ignores Walters when Walters tries to shake his hand. He smokes his cigarette and waits for Rooster.

» » »

Billy and Rooster played Junior A hockey together a few years back. It's what brought Billy to town. Rooster's lived here his whole life. The hockey team got Billy jobs in the off-season. That kept him around, that and the puck bunnies. Billy fucked enough of them over the years. Then Debbie came along and Billy went straight.

Straighter, at least. He stopped fucking so many puck bunnies and started drinking more.

Billy was twenty-two when he and Debbie married. The hockey was finished. He had his Grade 12. He had no reason not to stay in town, no reason not to get married and find a job. He worked construction for a while and then tried landscaping. He was a janitor at the high school for a couple years. But Debbie wanted him to move on to something better. Rooster tried to get him in at the beer store but management was skeptical. They already had one washed up drunk driving for them, they didn't need another. Debbie told Billy to try retail. So he did, mostly to keep her off his back.

Krazy Kevin's hired him on the spot. It was the second place he'd applied to. Krazy Kevin was a hockey fan. Walters told Billy that Krazy Kevin remembered him from his playing days.

Walters said, "We'll give you a shot, kid. Kevin says you got some profile in this town. That's just what we need. Profile."

Billy cut his hair, bought some collared shirts, neckties, and dress shoes and went to work selling TVs, stereos, radios, walkmans—you name it. He did a decent enough job, good enough that Krazy Kevin kept him around. He was right about Billy's profile, at least for a couple years. Customers recognized Billy. They shot the shit about the hockey team, shook Billy's hand and sometimes bought something from him. Billy put up with it. He did it for Debbie more than anything. But eventually the bullshit got to be too much.

» » »

Rooster pulls up in the beer store truck and Billy climbs into the cab. Rooster's got a king can open between his knees.
"Grab one."
"Cans? You don't need to drop bottles no more?"
"Don't worry about it. I got a system."
"Great. Thanks, Rooster."
Billy settles in and Rooster drives off on his rounds.
"So, what the fuck? You fuckn packin' this job in, Billy?"
"Yeah."
"Fuck for? It's a soft fuckn job."
"That's part of the problem. I got my reasons."
"So you say. But you always hated them hard jobs. Remember you tried to work construction? That didn't work out too fuckn good. What you gonna do now?"
"Get drunk."
Rooster laughs. "Oh yeah! You called the right fuckn man then my friend."
Billy and Rooster clank cans as the truck rolls to a stop beside the North Star Tavern, out Highway 7 at the edge of town.

"Debbie's gonna be pissed."

"Don't fuckn care. Debbie's always pissed. She's part of the problem."

"You working on a solution?"

"Might be."

"Back in ten."

Rooster grabs his work gloves off the dash and hops out of the cab.

Billy sits back and drinks his beer.

》》》》

Billy and Debbie live in a townhouse. They bought it a couple years ago. Billy'd saved a bit working at Krazy Kevin's. Debbie used to cut hair. She told Billy she wanted to quit, that she wanted to go back to school at the college and study interior decorating.

"The fuck's that?"

"What's it sound like?"

"Don't get fuckn smart."

"Billy, there's more money in it. Plus it's what I know I'm good at. It'll let me bring out my creative side. And I can get clients from my connections at the haircutter's."

"Eh? Fuck that. You're dreaming. You're good at cutting hair."

"Anyone can cut hair."

"So cutting hair's not good enough for you. That the problem?"

"Something like that."

Debbie quit her job. She started a couple decorating courses and then quit those too. She told Billy she didn't like riding the bus alone across town all the way to the college.

Soon Debbie got bored at home and went on a decorating kick. A couple months ago Billy came home from work and Debbie was hanging new drapes. A couple weeks later it was paint and wallpaper. Then new fixtures for the bathroom. Last week, new carpets throughout the townhouse—front hall, living room, the stairs, the two bedrooms upstairs—all covered with new wall-to-wall carpet.

"Who's fuckn paying for this, Debbie?"

"We are."

"We are? You mean I am."

"We're married, Billy. It's how it works. Besides, the carpets was on sale."

Billy snorted and looked at the carpets. "Fuckn colour is that? Who has snot green carpets in their house? That why they's on sale?"

"It's not green, it's called aquamarine."

"Eh? The fuck's that? That ain't a colour."

"It is so a colour. Aquamarine. Open a fuckn book once in a while, Billy."

Billy just looked at Debbie. He had nothing to say to that.

» » »

Billy's into his second king can when Rooster gets back in the truck.

"Got one more stop to make then we can get us some lunch."

"Foxx's Den?"

"Fuckn right. Throw me a pop."

Rooster cracks the beer, puts the truck in gear and away they go back down #7 and into town. He does his last stop quickly. Billy sits and drinks, listening to Rooster shuck cases of beer.

They sit right down front at the Foxx's Den.

"Two Blues and two lunch specials," Billy says to the waitress. He turns to Rooster. "Lunch's on me. Don't fuckn care if I can't afford it no more."

The beers arrive before the food. Billy and Rooster stare up into the lights.

"Nice rack," Rooster says, pointing with his beer at the stripper.

"Got that fuckn right. She look familiar to you Rooster? Like maybe she used to hang around the rink?"

They're both half cut now.

"The fuck should I know. It was hard to see their faces when their heads was bobbin' on the end of my cock."

Billy spits beer when he laughs. "Right. Forgot you liked the cum-chuggers."

"Cleaner than fuckn them Billy my friend."

"No doubt."

"So you give it up then, Billy? Quit the bunnies like you quit this job of yours?"

"Mostly. But the ones I know ain't bunnies no more. More like cougars."

"Right. But what you gonna do for a paycheque now you quit Krazy Kevin's? Cougars don't come cheap. Your wife don't come cheap."

Billy stares at the stripper. "Don't worry about me, Rooster. I'm a dreamer. Got plenty ah big plans."

Rooster scoffs, "No room for dreamers in this town."

"Maybe so but I got ideas."

The stripper finishes. Rooster looks at Billy. "How 'bout a table dance from her? To make you feel better after quitting your job and all."

"Sounds good. But not just for me. We'll share her. Like old times at the rink."

Rooster laughs. Billy waves the stripper over. She complies and goes into a lethargic dance for Billy and Rooster. She starts out wearing light blue bra and panties, a set that matches her eyes. Rooster notices. "Nice eyes on her."

Billy thinks he's joking at first. He's not been looking at her eyes.

"Nice eyes," Rooster says again, louder this time. "Nice and green." He might be playing games but the stripper is impressed he noticed. She takes off the bra and panties and drapes the panties over Rooster's head. Rooster keeps looking at her eyes.

Billy stops looking at her tits for a second and glances at her eyes. "You got a point, Rooster. She's a looker. Shame she's in this line of work."

The stripper looks insulted.

Billy says, "But those ain't green eyes, Rooster. That colour, it's called aquamarine."

"Don't care what it's called, Billy, it's the finest fuckn thing I seen all day."

The stripper turns her back to Billy and dances for Rooster, gently swaying her tits in his face while Rooster stares at her eyes. Billy does what he can with his view of her ass.

By the time she leaves, Billy and Rooster have paid for six table dances and bought her a couple eleven-dollar cocktails. They chatted her up for a while and let her take a break from the table dances. She told them she was from up north, Kapuskasing, but who knows. She said she came to town to study to be a real estate agent, that that's her ambition in life. Eventually, she left because she wanted to take a smoke break before her next floorshow. Billy and Rooster let her go.

They order more beers and stick around. They take in her second show, her third and fourth too. They're still there five hours later when she clocks out for the night. Rooster and Billy call her Aquamarine all afternoon and into the evening. She hears them say it from the front row when she dances. She likes the sound of it. It's a stage name she just might use. Real estate can wait.

» » »

Debbie's right pissed when Billy stumbles in at one-thirty. "The fuck you been? I made your favourite: fish sticks and cream corn."

Billy's so drunk he can barely stand.

"I said where you been, Billy? Don't fuckn call or nothing."

Billy looks at the cream corn. Favourite, my ass, he thinks. Stone sober it nearly makes him gag. Drunk it makes him sick straightaway. He pushes past Debbie toward the bathroom. He doesn't make it and vomits all over the carpet in the living room.

Debbie's on him. "Ah fuck. All over my new carpet. You shit, Billy. How old are you? Clean that shit up. It's gonna stain. It's gonna ruin the fuckn colour."

Billy wipes barf and drool from his chin. He's hunched over on his hands and knees, head spinning. He looks down at the carpet. "Aquamarine."

"Fuck's that, Billy? The fuck you say?"

"Aquamarine."

"Hey? Speak up."

"Aquamarine, not snot green. What colour underwear you got on, Deb?" Billy giggles to himself.

"You makin' fun, Billy? I'll show you fun." Debbie tramps over and kicks Billy in the ass. Billy just snorts and keeps on giggling, then all-out laughing.

"You're fuckt Billy, you're truly fuckt. Stop laughing and clean up that mess. I paid good money for these carpets."

"Aquamarine." Billy's laugh dies down. "But you're wrong, Debbie. You didn't pay for jack shit. You paid for nothing. I paid for this fuckn carpet and I don't like the colour. I don't like *aqua . . . ma . . . rine.*"

Billy lies on his back, staring at the ceiling. The plaster patterns swirl and dance. He hears Debbie stomping around in the kitchen. He starts to laugh. He laughs harder and harder. He laughs so hard that he pisses himself.

Debbie comes over and stands above him, hands on her hips. "You fuckn loser, Billy Arnason! You fuckn loser!"

Billy just lies there laughing.

Debbie stomps back to the kitchen and then comes at him with his dinner. She chucks it but misses. Fish sticks fly in every direction. The cream corn slops on the carpet, next to Billy's head. The dinner plate comes to a rest by the sofa.

"Fuck this shit," she says and storms out.

Billy rolls over and looks at the mess. He gets up slowly, his pant-legs soaked in urine. He unzips and steps out of his pants and kicks his underwear off. He scratches his head, goes to the kitchen for a beer and then back to the living room. He steps over his soiled pants and underwear, the cream corn and dinner plate. Then he slumps down on the sofa and tries to unwind. He should go after Debbie. It's too late for her to be out alone.

» » »

Suburban Pornography

Richardson's at it again. Fourth Saturday night in a row. I'm sitting here in relative peace and comfort in my modest suburban bungalow watching the Habs redefine mediocrity while he's across the street, distracting me, fucking up my leisure time again.

He's got the blinds up and the curtains open on the big bay window at the front of his house. He's got his big screen TV set dead centre in his living room so all the neighbours can see the images thereon. From my place I can see the screen perfectly. Richardson's even parked his sports car and SUV inside the big double garage, making sure there's no possible obstruction for me. How courteous. The bastard.

I grab a beer and take a hit, my eyes never leaving Richardson's TV. I can hear Harry Neale yammering in the background from my TV, something about the Habs' dreadful power-play record of late. I'm not bothered, even though they're playing the Leafs. I can watch the highlights later. The real action is about to take place across the street.

As he's done on past Saturdays, Richardson's fast-forwarding through a porno, getting a preview of the action. I watch blurred images of naked women and men fucking at break-neck speed, massaging the cold beer bottle in my left hand. Richardson hits play now and again, taking a closer look at this or that blonde or brunette, sucking this or that cock, and then it's back to bolting through the videotape. He's likely making mental notes for later: i.e., "there's when I make my first move," or "that'll be when she'll be really fired up, ready to go."

I shift my eyes away from the TV for a second. He's rewinding now anyway. I take a handful of pretzels out of the bag by my feet and let my eyes drift to the second storey of Richardson's place. There's his wife, right on cue. Through their upstairs hallway window I can see her slinking away from the baby's room, down the hall to the master bedroom. No shame. No self-respect.

In the master bedroom she flicks on the light, illuminating her silhouette. She turns sideways, starts disrobing, giving me a profile, like one of those old-fashioned cameos. I can see every curve and rounded mound this way. Fuck sakes. She's over at the lingerie drawer next. It's like I live there. Like I'm her damned husband. No secrets in that household. And I thought this would be such a quiet, clean and tidy neighbourhood, out here away from the grime and din in the city. All these perfectly normal, suburban middle-class folks lined up like ducks in their matching grey-brick houses.

Normal, my ass. These people are weirder than the miscreants downtown. Nothing normal about any of it. All a fucking façade. Closets brimming with skeletons. Look at Mrs. Richardson now, bent over, red thong riding up the crack of her plump ass, rummaging through the drawer of sex toys. Wonder what it'll be tonight? The riding crop? Transparent dildo? Butt plug? Maybe Richardson's glow-in-the-dark cock-ring with built-in clit stimulator? I'll know soon enough.

She's made her choice but her back's to me now. She turns, glides out of the master bedroom and heads downstairs for the main event. I rub my eyes for a second, making sure they're working okay. Making sure I'm not delusional. Everything's in working order. I can see *all* too clearly. I jump up from the couch. I'll need another beer, maybe two, for what follows.

» » »

I know where Richardson gets the movies. There's a place called the Naughty Mart in the strip mall at the end of the street. It's wedged between a Hortons and one of those First Choice haircutting places. Like it's nothing out of the ordinary. Like I said, normal. While the wife gets a trim you grab a coffee and then rummage through the new releases, fingering your favourite form of porn, making a selection. The twenty-one-year-old girl with a silver stud in her tongue working for minimum wage at the counter doesn't bat an eye when you give her the tag and she makes you sign for *Backdoor Bonanza* or *Where the Boys Aren't #18*.

After that—porn in hard—pick up the wifey and drive across the street to the big box stores. Do some groceries. Grab some supplies at Home Depot; maybe cruise through the electronics at Future Shop. Future, my ass. This is the *present*. Suburbanites racing around in vehicles that have more in common with tanks than cars, flaunting disposable incomes that baffle the mind, lusting after tax cuts, spending it all on entertaining themselves to death. And these, *these* are my neighbours. The Dorfmans. The Harveys. The Marcellinis. The O'Briens.

And then there's the Richardsons. Those purveyors of porn. Those suburban seducers. Those sex-hungry thirty-somethings. I've seen him coming and going from the Naughty Mart. I've been sitting in Hortons on a Sunday morning, reading the paper, when their SUV pulls up and out he jumps, slipping the video through the overnight return slot, feigning discretion, his chin nudged into his chest to obscure his face, baby in the car seat, the three of them on their way to the 9:30 service round the corner at St. John the Divine's. Fuck sakes. Sex slaves one day, genuflecting Christians the next. What can I say? Welcome to the suburbs, my friend.

» » »

They're about twenty minutes into the filth now. I'm on my third beer. Two more sit on the carpet at my feet, slowly warming, next to the empty bag of pretzels. In the background I hear that the second period just ended and the Habs are down 4-1. My, my, how things have changed. The first thirty years of my life the Leafs were whipping boys for the great and powerful Habs. Of course, that was a simpler era. Everything was straightforward and in its proper place. A time of order and discretion. Long before everything became so pornographic.

It's the second sex scene of whatever dreary movie they're watching across the street; I forget the title. A bronze-shouldered man with slicked black hair and a tongue like a cobra is making an Asian babe writhe in apparent ecstasy. His head is tilted left just so, her clit at the centre of the shot. This'll go on for a minute or two, then they'll switch roles and she'll pump his cock in her mouth for a while. Then it'll be on to the plundering penetration scenes and those frightful close-ups of various holes and hairy ass cheeks. Good thing I'm across the street. Then, finally, *his* sputtering climax—the cum shot, the money shot.

If the format is followed (and when isn't it?), sex scene #3 will be girl-on-girl action. Then, a threesome. The last segment should be something marginally kinky—a little spanking and black PVC undies. Although the Richardsons might not make it that far.

Propping myself up on an elbow, it looks like he's about to make his move. Oh Christ, he's peeling off the Y-fronts. Here comes the action. Richardson's an eager beaver tonight.

Pornography is one thing. It's typically vile and predictable on its own, harmless, mostly. But when regular suburban folks start mimicking pseudo-sex, a fine line is crossed. But still, I'm drawn to it. Like flies to shit. Fruit flies to sugar. That is, at least until I cum. Then it's on to feeling momentarily unclean, recognizing my subhuman behaviour for what it is: a base, uncontrolled urge that goes way beyond obsession and want. That's why I watch. Can't help myself. Can't take my eyes away, no matter how sickening and silly the neighbours' stunts are. It's Saturday night; I should be watching hockey, drinking beer and farting in my empty living room. But I need something, a fix to fill my void and anything remotely pornographic will do. This, this scene across the street is a cornucopia of depravity that strikes right to the marrow and fits snugly, like a condom on a very hard cock.

They're right into it now on their couch. A minute ago I glanced away; the Habs are down 6-1, which is too painful to watch. Mrs. Richardson has shed the red thong, her legs are parted, knees in the air, head thrown to one side, mouth puckered just so, eyes closed, while Richardson pounds away. And hey, he is wearing the glow-in-the-dark cock-ring after all.

The movie glides on behind them, the actors not bothered that they've lost their viewers. The Mrs. looks over at it once in a while, simulates a grunt or groan, like she's reading a teleprompter. Richardson bites her neck. Squeezes her shoulder. Sucks a nipple firmly between his lips, distending it. Takes up her hair in one fist and gently tugs. Spanks her thigh, fucks his wife with all the verve and virtuosity that a husband of ten years can muster.

"That a boy, Richardson. Hustle. Get it in there, big fella," I say out loud in my living room, concealing a snicker.

His face starts to contort. Her back starts to arch. The veins on his neck stand out like cables. Her toes curl. He's coming. I think she's faking it. A couple more plunges and he collapses like he's been shot with an elephant gun, rolling off her. She coos, rubbing her tits a little. Then leans over and kisses him on the top of his balding head, nuzzling in next to him, seeking warmth and comfort. This is followed by a post-coital cuddle to reassert their humanity. Welcome to the boring part. Time to check the final score and maybe listen to Don Cherry's post-game rant.

But I'm too late for Cherry. I've got Peter Mansbridge on screen instead. Fuck sakes. Nothing sexy about him.

I drain the dregs of my last beer, stand, and walk the empties back to the kitchen. I turn, head down a corridor to my first-floor washroom. Piss, shaking off my semi. Grab a bottle of hand lotion. Head back to the living room. Hit rewind on my video camera that's been focused in on my neighbours for the past two hours. Make the necessary mechanical manipulations. Then draw the drapes across my window. It'll be a private showing for me. I have some shame, some semblance of pride, respect for my neighbours, after all, despite living in this filthy suburb on the outskirts of town. Maybe Richardson should take note, but I fear he's beyond saving, in way too deep.

>> >> >>

Bruised Ribs

Jimmy Monahan sits on a park bench minding his own business, flipping through a magazine.

"Hey there. 'Scuse me. You got the time?"

The guy who said it walks up to Jimmy. The guy wears faded jeans, grey T-shirt, ball cap and a black leather jacket that's too small for him. He has a bulging knapsack on his back. A grubby, grey teddy bear hangs from a noose off his knapsack.

"It's about ten past one," Jimmy says. "I'm not wearing a watch, but it's about ten past one."

"That right? Shit. I thought it was at least five or six," the guy says.

"No, no. Nowhere near. It's just after one."

"Thanks. I had to be somewhere yesterday at two-thirty.

The doctor's. Nearly missed it. I coulda sworn now it was about five or six. I don't wear a watch neither."

The guy comes over and sits beside Jimmy on the bench. The guy winces when he sits and then gasps. He puts his knapsack on the bench slowly. Even more slowly, he reaches over and gently strokes the teddy bear's head.

"Bruised my ribs," he says.

"Oh yeah?" Jimmy rolls up his magazine.

"Yeah. Playing football with a bunch of fourteen- and fifteen-year-olds. Over in Hampton Park. You know it?"

"Yeah. Just east of here, right?"

The guy looks at Jimmy funny. "I guess. I don't know about east or west or that but it's near here somewheres."

The guy takes off his ball cap and wipes sweat from his forehead with his T-shirt. It's close to thirty degrees. It's way too hot to be wearing what he's wearing.

"Bruised, not cracked?" Jimmy asks.

"Yeah. Hurts like a son of a bitch. Doctor said I was lucky. Cracked ribs they woulda hadtah examine my lungs and shit. I got off easy with just a couple X-rays."

"Tackle football?"

"Yeah."

"With kids?"

"Yeah. But they were built, like. Solid kids. Fuck, twenty-five years younger than me. They gang-tackled me. Piled on, the pricks. What was I doing? What was I thinking? Wasn't thinking. Don't think enough before I do stuff."

"Been a long time since I played tackle football."

"You're smart. Last time I do it. I thought first, hey, let's play flag football. Remember that? Flag football? Put those little red flags in your belt and away yah go. No one gets hurt. But no, these punks wanted to play tackle. 'Flag football,' they said; 'you mean *fag* football.' What choice did I have then, eh?"

Jimmy riffles the closed pages of his magazine with his thumb. "What were you doing playing football with them in the first place?"

"They asked, that's why. I was there, just hanging around the park. They was short or something. I had fuck all else to do. Was just sitting in the park like you're doing now. You know how it happens sometimes."

"That right?"

"Yeah, that's right."

"And sometimes you end up with bruised ribs."

"Yeah. Sometimes. Something like that. I guess."

Jimmy edges over to the guy. "But what are bruised ribs? I mean, ribs are bone. How do you bruise ribs exactly?"

"I told you already—playing tackle football with fourteen- and fifteen-year-old kids. Solid kids. Try it some time, you'll see what I mean."

The guy sounds annoyed. He puts his ball cap back on and stands to leave. He picks up his knapsack and then grabs his ribs like he's having a heart attack. The grey teddy bear dangles from its noose.

"Fuck it hurts, man. Shit sakes." He catches his breath and then carries on, "But thanks for the time. That really helps me out."

"No problem," Jimmy says. "You want help with anything else?"

"No, no, you've done enough. You've given me plenty to think about. That'll keep me on an even keel. Take 'er easy."

"You too."

"Yeah, thanks," the guy says with a grunt. And away he goes.

Jimmy watches the guy walk away. Then he sits on the bench for a minute, drumming one knee with his balled-up magazine. He looks up in the sky and assesses the angle of the sun, trying to figure if his estimation of the time is accurate. He looks over at the play structure to his left in the park. There are no little kids on it. They're off having afternoon naps. Teenagers hang out on it instead, five or six of them who should be in school. They smoke, their bodies drooped. One of them toes the woodchips that surround the play structure. They look about fourteen, fifteen years old.

Jimmy watches them for a few minutes and then gets up and walks across the park to his house. He tosses the magazine on a lawn chair. He goes into the garage and rummages around, pulling out a half-inflated football. Jimmy tosses it in the air, catches it and smiles to himself.

He played high school football. Jimmy was the quarterback of his junior team but got beat out for the position in senior by a kid with a stronger arm. He played defensive back in senior. It rankles him to this day. Jimmy is convinced he got screwed. The other kid had a good arm but couldn't keep the plays straight. Jimmy gave it up after high school.

Jimmy steps out on the street and tosses the ball higher in the air. He catches it, tucks it under his arm, feigns a straight-arm and deke, then laughs to himself. Jimmy turns on his heel and goes back to the park.

The teenagers are playing hacky-sack. Jimmy walks up to them.

"Hey, you guys you wanna throw the ball around?"

The teenagers give him indifferent or weird looks. Their faces say, "Who the fuck is this old fart and what the fuck does he want?"

Jimmy smells pot smoke. "Come on. Let's toss the old pigskin around." He throws the ball in the air again, takes two quick steps and catches it. He smiles at the teenagers.

"Come on buddy," Jimmy says, pointing the ball at one guy. "Go deep. I've got the arm for it. I'll hit you right in the numbers." Jimmy drops back in an imaginary pocket, scanning the field for an open receiver.

The kids go back to playing hacky-sack, except for one. The kid Jimmy pointed the ball at steps toward Jimmy. "No thanks, man. Listen, we just be, like, chillin.' Too hot to be running around." He's got his hands in his pockets, his back scrunched, hair in his eyes.

Jimmy tries again. "Come on lads. A little football. You guys know how to play football, right?" He tucks the ball in like a fullback and makes like he's going to plough into the kids.

The same guy who talked talks again. "Listen, man, thanks but no thanks. We just be not into it. You know what I'm sayin'?"

Jimmy feels a rush of anger. He's pissed at how the kid is talking to him. His face reddens. He blurts, "Okay! Okay you lazy faggots! Kick your stupid fuckn beanbag around instead."

Then Jimmy turns and punts the ball. It doesn't travel far, hardly bounces, being low on air.

The kid who talked to Jimmy shakes his head and goes over to the hacky-sack game. Another kid sparks a fresh joint. One kid says, "What be his fuckn problem?"

Jimmy waves a hand at them in disgust. Then he goes down in a three-point stance, holds it for a second before bursting up and charging at the ball. He jumps on it as if a phantom opponent fumbled the ball. Jimmy rolls over on his shoulder and leaps back up on his feet. He sprints with the ball under his arm, dodging left and right in the grass to an invisible end zone. When Jimmy gets there, he spikes the ball, turns and looks at the teenagers. He does a victory dance and then gives the kids the finger, even though none of them look at him. Then Jimmy falls on his back and stares at the clear sky. He slips the half-inflated ball under his head like a pillow.

"Kids today," he snorts to himself. "Stupid as a bag of hammers. Lazy bunch of jackasses."

Jimmy thinks this sounds funny. He wraps his arms around his middle and laughs and laughs until his eyes water, until his sides feel like they're going to split.

» » »

The Last Time

I'm watching Brenda dress for what might be the last time. She takes off her bathrobe and tosses it on the bed beside me. I feel its dampness through the thin cotton sheet. She turns to the closet. Black hair hangs down across her naked back. She rummages in her underwear basket, removing a white pair. Bends at the waist slightly, lifts her left foot, then her right and pulls them up snug around her ass. She snaps the hem, smoothes her underwear across each cheek.

A white bra to match. One arm through, the other, the bra rests across her breasts. She reaches behind—her shoulder blades bending in toward each other—and fastens the clasp.

Next, white knee-high stockings. This always gets my attention. I prop up slightly on one elbow. Often, I'd masturbate to this: to either her image after she left, or, if she'd indulge me, to her while she pulled the stockings up and smoothed them across her calves. But not this morning. Brenda bends one knee, slides a stocking on; repeats with the other leg.

Then she stands back, facing the full-length mirror on the back of the bedroom door. Hands on her hips. Tilts her head to the right. Admires herself. She shifts her gaze, looking over her right shoulder at me. She doesn't smile. She is beautiful but there is sadness and sorrow in her ritual this morning.

Her outerwear requires no thought: white nurse's scrubs. She steps into the pants and pulls them up. She knots the ties at the front firmly. The top over her head. She pulls it down over her hips as far as it will go. Again she steps in front of the full-length mirror. She levels the crisp, white uniform across her torso. She bends and pulls her stockings up as far as they will go. She doesn't like them to droop. Bent over, I see panty lines through the white material of her scrubs.

Next, Brenda takes her hair in both hands and fastens it into a tight ponytail with an elastic fixed with yellow beads: the only splash of colour on her otherwise snowy uniform. Then she grabs her ID badge off the dresser—her tired work photo on the front next to the logo of the hospital—and pins that to her breast pocket. She steps into white Nike trainers that she never ties, or ties about once a week.

Brenda is so pristine, beautiful and efficient-looking that I want to cry. I want to reach out and pull her down on the bed, loosen her hair, draw her in next to me and muddy her pristine beauty. But I know she won't have it. And it's the sort of impulse that gets me in trouble, got me here this morning. I grab hold of the hem of her wet bathrobe instead and wait for her to speak, to say anything to me.

She has not spoken all morning. Despite last night's fury, we shared our bed as usual, although she slept turned away from me. In the morning, she rose and headed straight for the bathroom. I lay alone and watched daylight enter the quiet room, the only noises were those coming from the bathroom: Brenda peed and flushed, showered, dried her hair, clanged about with makeup and then brushed her teeth.

On a normal day, I'd get up five minutes after her and join her in the bathroom. I'd sit on the toilet and talk to her while she showered. Or drop my pyjamas and shower with her, lather her in soap, scrub her, wash her hair and massage her scalp—fuck standing while the hot water doused us both. But this is not a normal day and I dared not move from bed.

Fully dressed for work, Brenda takes her keys off the

dresser. She'll grab her knapsack from the front hall on the way out. She catches the bus on the corner at 6:35 to start her shift at 7. She pulls back the bedroom door, obscuring the full-length mirror. She rattles her keys, then stops and regards me on the bed.

"I want you out by the time I'm home from work. No exceptions. No discussion this time. Just gone. For good."

It's what I was expecting. Stronger than before. I've pushed too far.

I swallow hard, try to summon a reply but before I can, she's gone.

A couple minutes later, aware she's halfway to the bus stop, I call out, "Brenda? Brenda, hang on." It's pointless, I know. Still, I holler. "Brenda, wait! You're not serious. Wait. What'll you do without me? Brenda."

Later, I get out of bed and walk to the bathroom. I stand and pee in the small, quiet room. Then flush. I lean over the sink where a pair of Brenda's underwear soaks in tepid water. I stare at the obscured pattern of yellow flowers on the material under water. Then I knuckle my eyeballs, go make coffee and phone Alice. Or maybe it's too early for that.

>> >> >>

On a Quiet Residential Street

Sam Marconi drives his small car slowly up his quiet, residential street. There she is again. She's got her back to him, wearing just a bra. She's hunched over an ironing board.

Sam stops just past her house. He gets out of his car and stands in the street. It's dark and there is no one around. It's just past ten o'clock. Everyone on the street is tucked away in their safe, quiet houses.

"Fuck it. I'm doing it tonight."

Sam walks up the walkway to her house. He steps into the garden under the living room window and raps on the glass. She stops ironing and looks over her bare shoulder at him. She pauses and then puts down the iron.

"Get over here, tease."

When she turns, Sam sees she has nice, round tits. Her bra is black. He always thought she'd be in panties but she's wearing a skirt. It has a simple, plaid pattern.

Holy fuck. Just look at her.

She walks over, opens the window and speaks first, calmly. "I've seen you before. What took you so long?"

"I had to be sure," Sam says.

"Sure? Sure of what?"

"Listen, this isn't normal, you gotta realize that."

"Normal? What's normal for this street? All sorts of weird shit goes on behind the walls of these houses, believe me."

She stands with her back straight. With all the lights on in her living room, she is fully visible to anyone passing by. But no one passes by.

She goes on, "You're going to have to be quiet. My husband is sleeping. He works midnights. He sleeps through everything, but he'll be up like clockwork at eleven."

"Your husband is a stupid man to be sleeping at a time like this," Sam says.

"Maybe so. But that's him; asleep at the wheel."

"You wanna screw around on him to punish him?"

"Punishment has nothing to do with it. This is for me."

She runs the palm of her left hand over the top of her left breast, where the skin is not covered by black material.

Sam inches forward. He says, "You're doing it for you? Well then, you're going about it in a screwy sort of way. What's with the ironing? You wanna fuck around, why not just go to the bars?"

"Too obvious. I want subtlety."

"Subtlety? You the sensitive type?"

"I'm a woman."

"No shit. Nothing subtle about that." Sam's eyes drop to the black bra and lower, to her stomach and then to the hem of her plaid skirt. His feet have sunk into the earth in the garden. He steps forward and tries to clamber up to the windowsill.

"No, no. Not so fast. Wait until you're invited," she says.

"What am I, a vampire?"

"I don't know what you are. But this goes at my pace."

"Look, we keep this up, someone is gonna see. Some nosy asshole will look out their window and see it all. This is a quiet street. But they'll see you. See my car. Put two and two together. You know what they're like around here."

She fires back, "Do you think I care about the neighbours? I've been ironing like this for ages. The old guy across the street jacks off behind his drapes whenever I iron. Same with the teenaged kid in the house next to the old guy. Only the kid's got a telescope on me. He knows every mole and blemish on my back. I don't care about them. They're cowards. They're stuck in their houses afraid to come out. But you; I've seen you drive by. I've seen you slow down. I've seen you stop and stare. You've never jacked off but I've seen you sit in your car and watch. This is the first time you've come up to the window. It's about time. I was starting to wonder. Starting to wonder whether you're a coward too."

Sam takes a look out at the street. He looks for the old man, for the kid. He doesn't see anything apart from pulled drapes, closed curtains and dim lights behind. Then he looks past her to the ironing board. "But I don't get it. Seriously, what's with the ironing? How can someone iron every night?"

"It's a compulsion. I go to bed and see my husband lying there sleeping. I'm tired but I can't lie down with him. I can't stand the thought of seeing him in that mess of blankets and sheets. I think of all the sheets, towels, skirts, shirts, pants in the house and all their wrinkles. I have to leave the room."

Sam looks at her and shakes his head. "Alright, but why do you take your top off?"

"I like the feel of the hot iron in my hand, the heat, the steam. I like my shoulders bare. And I want someone to notice."

"It worked."

She stares down at Sam. Then she punches out the window screen. "Get in here."

Sam climbs up onto the windowsill. He kicks off his shoes into the garden behind him and then falls through the window. He flops down on the floor with a thud. He jumps up. They both stand and listen for the husband. Not a peep. She reaches down and opens his pants. They fall down around his ankles. His cock is hard. It bobs about as she leads him to the sofa. He kicks his pants off and leaves them on the carpet in a crumpled pile. She turns and takes off his shirt, unbuttoning it slowly. Then she points to the sofa.

"Sit."

Sam sits in his underwear on the sofa, watching her. She picks up his pants from the floor. She turns her back to Sam and stands erect over the ironing board in her black bra and plaid skirt. She irons his pants and shirt. She folds them and places them on the windowsill. Then she turns to him. "You can go now. We're done. My husband will be awake soon."

Sam's jaw drops. "What the? What the fuck?"

"You heard me. Put these on outside, in the garden. Not in here."

"Fuck that. I mean, you're half naked. You invite me in here and take my clothes off. What the fuck?"

He wants to lunge at her, wrestle her to the ground, rip off her skirt and fuck her. She presses a button on the iron and a gasp of steam shoots out. Then she points to a clock on the wall: five minutes to eleven.

Sam stares at her and shakes his head. "You're fucked, you are truly fucked."

"Don't talk like that or I won't have you back," she says.

"Back, are you nuts?"

"You decide. You know where to find me." She turns away and starts ironing.

Sam sighs, walks over to the window and climbs out. He dresses in the garden. He walks to his car and stands beside it. He looks back at the house but he doesn't see her. The curtains are drawn and the lights are out, the same as nearly every other house on the block. He pauses and then looks down at his pants, runs a hand across the material of his shirt. He bends his right knee. He reaches down and feels the crisp crease in his pants. Sam opens the door to his car and gets in, careful not to wrinkle anything. He drives off and circles round the block to his place.

He parks his car in the street and looks at his house. The curtains are drawn and the lights are out. Sam kicks the curb and then goes to the side of the house to take the garbage out to the street. He turns next and looks up the street to where she lives before heading inside and up to the bedroom.

Sam stands beside the bed for a moment. His wife, Emily, sleeps. Sam takes off his shirt and pants. He balls them up and tosses them in a heap in the laundry hamper in the corner of the room. He gets into bed and nudges in next to Emily. Sam wraps his left arm around her middle. He has a hard-on. He presses it into the crack of her ass and rubs up against her, but Emily does not stir.

》 》 》

A Serious Deterrent

Eddie's cell phone rings right when he brings the first rye and Coke of the night to his lips. He doesn't drink. The phone rings again. Third call in the last twenty minutes. He was just on it when he stepped into Puzzles—a cheesy cougar bar in the west end—for a quick drink.

Another ring.

The phone sits on the bar, vibrating on the fake wood when it rings.

He hesitates, hand visibly trembling as his brain juggles options: quick drink or answer the phone? Ice rattles in his glass. Stress is killing him, he's sure of it.

The phone rings again, grating.

Eddie looks past his drink at the bartender. A cliché, he's rubbing a highball glass with a tea towel. He's got a bead on Eddie and can't wait to see what he'll do next, where the phone call might lead.

It rings again. Eddie almost drops his glass, spilling precious millilitres of drink on the bar's lacquered top. It's no mystery who's calling. Eddie doesn't need to check the display.

Another ring. That's six.

Bob the Bartender raises his eyebrows. If he weren't blessed with the sacred right to pour drinks, Eddie'd leap across the bar and throttle him.

Another fucking ring, seven.

Eddie's brain shifts gears. He grabs the drink and slugs it back in two gulps, pounding the empty glass down on the bar like he's playing a frat boy drinking game and snatches the phone, jamming the small device next to his big head.

"What?!"

"Eddie, that you? I can barely hear you. Where you at?"

"Who else this gonna be? You haven't figured out cell phones yet?"

"Don't get belligerent with me."

Her voice is weak, as usual.

"You've not seen the start of it."

"You sound different is all," she rasps.

Eddie looks over at the barkeep, points at his empty glass. The bartender gives him a slow, arrogant nod, folds his tea towel just so and places it on the bar. Then he pours Eddie another. It's a mistake. Eddie won't be able to savour this one either.

"What'dya want Shelley?"

"Well . . ." she starts.

He knows this won't be good, so he cuts her off, just as his fresh drink clinks in front of him.

"Cyril fuck off again? Leave you there to take care of your own self? Let me guess, you've pissed yourself. No wait, you've lost the TV converter in the sofa cushions. You need a pack of smokes from the store. Orange juice to wash down your meds. Am I getting close?"

There's an edge to Eddie's voice. Shelley's his sister but this is getting out of hand.

"Edward, dear."

Bang! Visions of their departed mom flash through his head. She was famous for starting sentences the same way, whenever she, too, had an annoying request.

"It's just . . ." Hack. Cough. Shelley gobs into her barf bowl. "Well . . ."

"Come on, Shell. Spit it out." Eddie clutches his drink in his left hand.

"Cyril had to go out, right. He had a meeting and so . . . so I'm all alone. Can't call the health visitor at this hour and, well . . ."

"Shelley, you just called me ten minutes ago, remember?"

She grunts, says yeah.

"You asked for a coffee from Hortons. Large. Milk,

three sugars. Right? I said sure. Said I'd be by in fifteen minutes. Said I had one stop to make first. Then you called back five minutes later and said to get some sourdough Timbits. Like I'm some pimply-faced punk in a drive-thru window. You remember any of this?"

"Edward, dear, don't get belligerent."

Eddie pauses, backs off a bit. "Sorry, Shell. It's the stress. It's eatin' me up—killin' me, I swear."

"Eddie, I wouldn't bother you but Cyril got called away to a meeting. He—"

Eddie cuts her off.

"Come on, Shell. Cyril's got no fuckn meeting. It's Friday night, just past midnight. What kind of a meeting do you think he's going to at this hour?"

She sputters, "Well, he told me he had to go downtown to his office to meet with . . I forget the name but he took his briefcase. Some papers. He's in the government, Eddie."

"The hell he is, Shell. Cyril's a low-rank civil servant is all, hardly makes him government."

"But he said it was government business. A government meeting. I'm sure that's what he said."

"Listen, Shell. I don't think that's the sorta meeting Cyril has in mind. We've been over this a thousand times. You gotta wise up. Cyril's fucking around, I'm sure of it."

"Edward, dear, please don't talk about Cyril that way." She hacks, like she's coughing up part of a lung, goes on. "He provides for me. Takes care of me."

Eddie feels the stress building again. He slugs back the second drink like his first. Two quick swallows. It helps. He starts to settle. Calmly, he talks into the phone. "We'll see about Cyril. But let's just forget about him for now. Worry about you instead. Somebody has to. Might as well be me."

The bluster has come out of him. Eddie feels like an ever-pleasing kid. A subservient civil servant, like Cyril.

"Sourdough Timbits, remember, Edward."

"Yeah, I remember. I'll be right over. Got your best interests at heart, Shell, I swear it."

"Thanks, Eddie. You're a dear."

An image of the ghost of his mother flashes at him for a second. Then Bob the Bartender gives Eddie the you-wanna-another look. Eddie nods. Knocks this one back fast too. Then puts a twenty on the bar and turns away. He walks towards the street, the phone still by his ear, Shelley's hacking and coughing bouncing off a satellite.

» » »

Outside it's snow-crunching, snot-freezing cold. Ottawa cold. Like seventy-five per cent of this white-collar town, Eddie's not native. The mind-numbing, minus-thirty stuff takes getting used to.

Eddie peers down Richmond Road toward his car. Nobody around. He should do like the rest of Ottawa and just stay indoors till April. He moved up here six years ago from Hamilton: Steeltown, home of the Tiger-Cats, mobsters, and the birthplace of Tim Hortons Donuts. He saw on the news the other day Sheila Copps launched her ill-fated leadership bid in a doughnut shop, hoping to capture the proletariat's imagination.

A woman led Eddie to Ottawa. Woman X. Back in Hamilton, Eddie worked crappy jobs, going nowhere and she got a sniff of the big time, was offered a job in the high-tech sector when the boom was on. She had taken some courses in holiday and hotel something or other at the local community college. Got a job booking trips for the suits at Corel.

Well, I guess fuckers like that can't be expected to make their own travel plans. Sounds like a sweet deal for you. Let's do it, Eddie said at the time.

So Eddie and Woman X hitched a U-Haul trailer to their Ford Escort and motored up to the nation's capital, deluded into thinking they'd prosper. Eddie's sister—Shelley—had moved up years before. She'd followed a man: the aforementioned Cyril. He'd rooted out a secure job in the federal government, an accountant in some Ministry, minding the public purse-strings. Shelley'd follow him to the end of the earth.

Everything was hunky-dory for Eddie and Woman X for the first two years. Then the missus got sacked, the slump hit, company went sour; there were no more trips to book.

Woman X started counting on Eddie to bring in some coin. Her first mistake. Eddie'd switched crap jobs in Hamilton for crap jobs in Ottawa. Amazing how there's no shortage of shitty, minimum-wage work no matter where you go. He washed dishes for a while. Drove for a courier for a few months. Variety store clerk, but that was just too embarrassing for someone pushing forty.

The latest gig is cleaning government offices downtown—Sunday to Thursday, straight nights. Eddie has lasted more than a year so far.

But minimum wage wasn't Woman X's idea of fun. Plus the marriage was beyond sour—rotten. Eddie'd lost interest, was indifferent. Woman X had had enough of his limp-dick antics and pissed off back to the Hammer, leaving Eddie to his own devices. He had no reason to follow. And about that time Shelley's health started to fall off. Eddie felt obligated to help; knew she couldn't count on Cyril. That guy's grated on Eddie's nerves for years. He's been watching Cyril's bullshit stunts, getting more and more irritated.

» » »

Ottawa's not a lunch-bucket town. It's a poppy-seed bagel and carrot sticks in a fanny pack kind of place. There's a few rough spots around Mechanicsville and Lower Town but mostly it's a quiet, unthreatening city, a metaphor for the entire country. And Ottawa's been a bit slow to catch the Tim Hortons wave. In Hamilton you can parachute down from the heavens and be guaranteed you'll land within half a kilometre of the caffeine and sugar Mecca. Ottawa, you have to go searching.

But Eddie found a Timmy's up on Carling a month or so ago, a mini-Hortons that's part of a gas bar. The car could use some fuel, so he heads that way.

Inside, some dude just out of high school gets Shelley's coffee and timbits. He's got the latest punk rip-off act blasting, trying to waken the dead hours of the night shift. Silver hoop pierces his eyebrow. Another in his lower lip. Greasy hair, zits.

He hands Eddie change. Eddie hesitates for a second. Then starts jawing with the kid.

"You like this shift?"

"Not too bad. Could be worse. Pays the bills."

The standard reply. Kid knows the lingo. Cynical beyond his years.

"Get many people coming in here this time of night?"

"Enough. Usually dead between two and five. A few weirdoes, maybe. The owners make me do other stuff. Clean up and shit."

"You always work alone?"

"Yeah . . . Hey, where you going with this shit?"

Eddie leans across the counter, breathing booze on the kid. "Just making conversation." He steps back and jingles the change in his pocket. "It was me, I'd, like, get some company in here and party. You know, some pussy."

Eddie doesn't know where this came from. Hearing the music, looking at the kid twenty years younger than him, Eddie must feel a sudden need to prove himself, to show he's still got something going on.

The kid snorts.

"I'm talking about a girl or two," Eddie goes, to clarify, to set the record straight. "Have a few drinks. Eat some of this shit food. Get all hyped up on sugar. See where it leads. You know, party. They still call it that, right?"

The kid gives Eddie a squirrelly look, like the idea never crossed his mind. Instead of sounding cool, Eddie sounds like a desperate, horny old fuck. The kid likely thinks Eddie's coming on to him. Eddie gives him a wink and then shuffles toward the door with the coffee and timbits.

Outside in the cold, Eddie shakes his head, trying to clear the cobwebs. He climbs back into the car and drives to his sister's.

» » »

Since Woman X pissed off, Eddie's not been fucked. The last year or so she was around they never fucked at all. That's more than two years without getting properly laid. Since she left he's been wanking off to shitty porno mags and videos. He's tried with some of the cougars at Puzzles.

Made out on a couple occasions half-heartedly in his car but he couldn't take it further.

There's a woman at work that he's also chased, mostly out of boredom and sheer desperation. She's a married mother of three rug-rats who likes to drink gin on the job, taking hits from a bottle hidden in her cleaning cart. Cheryl. She's flirted with Eddie since day one.

Eddie cornered her one night in the custodian's closet and thrust a thumb at his hard-on, subtle-like.

"That's from watching you all night bent over with that thing."

She laughed drunkenly and waved a feather duster in his face, gin on her breath, noticeable even at arm's length. Eddie made a grab for her and pulled her in close. She didn't resist.

"You can do what you want but I ain't taking nothing off. You're in charge of that. Ain't touching you nowheres neither," she slurred. "But you'll owe me for it."

Cheryl did a French maid routine; bent over and pretended to feather dust bleach bottles on a bottom shelf, showing Eddie her big, round arse.

"Go for it," she slurred.

She had on grubby pink sweats. Eddie grabbed them at the hem and yanked, exposing oversized panties. He tugged those down too without resistance. Cheryl just dusted away—unbothered—her pasty white ass pointed at the ceiling. Eddie pulled out his cock and beat himself silly, eyes tattooed on her butt cheeks—he's always been an ass man. It was the most intimate he'd been with a woman in a long time. He came in his fist, some of it dribbling onto the floor in the custodian's closet.

"Finished honey?" She held out her hand, waiting to be paid.

Eddie snarled, "You expect me to pay for *that*? I did it myself for fuck sakes."

She went all doe-eyed.

Eddie barked at her, "Put it in your mouth next time and I'll pay you, you old slut. Better yet, let me stuff it up that fat ass of yours."

"Suit yourself, Romeo. But that, that'll cost yah. And *you* can clean that up," she said, pointing the feather duster at the cum smear. Cheryl shrugged and pushed past him, back out to the grey office wasteland. There would be no next time.

» » »

Eddie also used to work the cleaning job with Craig Webb. Craig was part of the revolving door of cleaners. Lots of folks couldn't stand the nights, the tedium, or were just biding their time till they got better work. Craig was one of those. An ex-cop, he lasted about five months before moving on to something else. Eddie befriended him early on. They often passed the early morning hours shooting the shit about everything under the sun. Eddie had an eye for talent. Something told him Craig might come in handy one day.

Like Cheryl, Craig also fancied a drink or eight during working hours. One night he was oiled up and started talking to Eddie about his police work over a bottle of Canadian Club. The two of them leaned on their mop handles.

"Yeah, spent seven years on the provincial force."

"Long time. Whereabouts?" Eddie asked him.

"West ah here. Central Hastings Detachment. Out Marmora way. Down Highway 7."

"How was that?"

"Had a sweet deal. Till I fucked it all up."

"That right?"

Eddie kept his interventions short. Let Craig spill his guts.

"Used to spend my time—the winters anyways—busting drunk snowmobilers. They're fuckn ape-shit for it out there in those butt-fuck towns. Thought if they were on a snow-machine we'd leave 'em be. But enough of thems ended up dead we got word to clamp down. They didn't like it much. Cops weren't too popular among the townsfolk of Marmora, Madoc, or those sorta shit-holes."

Eddie nodded at him. "Something go wrong?"

"You got that right, ace." Craig knocked back a hit of rye. "But not with the snowmobilers. Had those pussies under our thumbs. Or so we thought. Trouble was in town.

Marmora. We'd be called in to break up domestics, bar fights, that kinda shit. Most ah the time it went off without too much bother. Some guy and his old lady tearing at each other's throats one minute, kissing and making up the next. But this one guy—fuck—this one prick really got under my skin. Randy Robertson. He'd get all liquored up and then start beating on his missus. That didn't bug me—she wasn't much to look at to start. Lippy cunt, too."

Craig stopped for a minute and stared hard at Eddie. Searched his eyes for something, before continuing.

"Don't knows about you, but I can do without lippy cunts. Know what I mean, mate?"

Eddie didn't know but pretended he did—smiling and nodding.

"So this time I decided to teach them Robertsons a lesson. It was April, but cold, and I didn't like the idea of being rushed out to help these two dumb fuckers sort out their differences. So we get there and the guy's more pissed than I've seen him before. Fucker can barely stand. But she's railing at him good. I asked what the problem was and she says, 'Dumb fuck tried to rape me.' 'That so,' I says."

Eddie leaned in close, inhaling Craig's boozy scent as the story built, tightening his grip on a mop handle.

"And she says, 'Fuckn right he did.' And I says, 'Anyone'd rape you oughta have his head examined.' Well, then the fireworks started. The husband suddenly sobers up and attacks me. So does the wife. Partner grabbed the bitch. But the drunk, he fuckn nailed me with a left hook. Came out of nowhere, right? One minute he can barely stand, the next he's swinging like Mike Tyson. Anyways, that fuckn did it for me. No one punches me and gets away with it. Uniform or not, I was gonna fuck the guy up good."

Craig stopped his story, momentarily cautious. Then his bravado got the better of him. "So we took the fucker to the Crowe River there in town and chucked him into the drink. How was I supposed to know he couldn't swim? Dumb prick. And the water was cold. Ice off it a week or two. Robertson almost died. My partner had the wife in the backseat of the cruiser. Her shrieking woke half the town. Another unit showed up on the scene and had to rescue the cocksucker from the river. I tried to weasel out from under it. Said he jumped when I was in pursuit on foot. But that didn't add up. Seems they had witnesses said they saw me drive him to the bridge. Said they saw me toss him over. Five, six witnesses. Turns out they were pissed-off snowmobilers. The season had just ended. They wanted to see a cop's ass fry. I got kicked off the force. Nearly criminal charges but the union saved me from that. Cut me a deal saying I'd never do police work again. I landed on my feet here in Ottawa."

A few seconds later, Eddie said, "Shit, some story. But cleaning work? How'd you end up in this hole?"

Craig snorted. "Better than keeping the peace in the market. I tried one of those bouncer jobs. Too much hassle. The owner kept trying to pawn slutty bartenders on us. I wasn't into that. I want a paycheque, not a blowjob from some young tart."

Eddie nodded again. Craig was spilling his guts all over the place. He took the bottle and polished off the contents, then said, "One reason I joined the force in the first place was to get away from skirts, if you know what I mean."

Again, Eddie didn't but pretended he did.

Calmly, just above a whisper, Craig summed up with, "Things could get pretty quiet in a police cruiser out Highway 7 in the middle of butt-fuck nowheres. Guy's gotta have something to do those cold winter nights. Gotta have something to take the edge off, right? That's another reason them drunk snowmobilers didn't like us much. Seems they weren't too crazy about me and my partner's cocks up their cold asses. But that little stunt we played right. Made damned sure there wasn't a fuckn witness within miles."

Eddie looked hard at Craig. Thought on what he'd said.

>> >> >>

When Eddie gets to Shelley's place she's facedown on the living room carpet. She lives in a townhouse, just off

Carling. The place reeks of piss—like a senior citizen's apartment, but Shelley's only forty-eight. She's on the floor, stirrup pants unhitched at the heels. At the top, her pants are pulled halfway down to her knees, urine soaking her underwear, the carpet, a little pooling on the battered hardwood.

"Fuck sakes," Eddie says, putting a hand over his nose. Shelley moans from the floor.

"Where's your bedpan? He didn't have the decency to set you up before he fucked off?"

Shelley doesn't answer. She's helpless; looks like fresh roadkill in the middle of her living room. Eddie's got no choice. He starts doing what he's done at least ten times the last few months. First he sets down the coffee and timbits and then leans over and picks up his frail sister, carries her into the bathroom and places her gently in the cold tub. He strips off her soiled clothes and turns on the shower. Shelley squeals when the water hits, lying there like a nearly dead carp. Eddie gets her meds from the kitchen counter. A glass of water. Holds her nose. Forces her to swallow. She starts to cry and splutter. It's hard on Eddie's nerves but he's got no choice.

Five minutes later he gets her out, towels her off and carries her down the hallway to the bedroom. He puts her naked on the bed, shifts her a little, setting a bedpan under her, then pulls up the crocheted blankets around her skinny frame and leaves her in her drugged state.

Eddie heads back to the living room and makes like Mr. Clean, wiping up the piss, cleaning the carpet as much as he can, the sulphurous odour no longer bothering him. Then he tosses Shelley's clothes in the wash and sets it to soak. When he's done he goes into the kitchen and gets a bottle of Cyril's, makes himself an extra large rye and Coke, grabs a handful of Timbits and parks himself in front of Shelley's tube. He passes two hours watching infomercials and chat-line adverts, slowly getting drunk. A couple times he's tempted to call one of the lines, his cock stiffening at the thought. He resists the urge.

Cyril still hasn't come home when Eddie leaves just after three. Must be some meeting, Eddie thinks, slamming his car into gear, tires clawing for purchase on the icy street.

» » »

Driving drunk—back out on Carling—Eddie grabs his cell and calls Craig. They've stayed in touch.

"Craig? Eddie. How's it hangin'? Gotta favour to ask. Got time for a coffee?"

"Edward, dear, good to hear from you. A favour? Fuck sakes, sounds sweet."

"I'll make it worth your while, as those pussies say on TV." Eddie runs a red. Nobody around, though.

"I'm liking the sound of this. Where you at?" Craig asks.

"Carling. Somewheres near Woodroffe."

"Okay. Gimme me fifteen minutes. Get us coffees and then meet me in the parking lot outside Canadian Tire. Got one stop to make first."

"Good. See you then."

Eddie tosses the cell on the passenger seat and turns the car around, heads back towards the Hortons at Carling and Maitland.

» » »

Craig did move on to something better after the cleaning job. He hooked up with a rent-a-cop home security outfit that wasn't put off by his indiscretions in Marmora. Craig came clean at the interview. Came across as the repentant type, showed remorse for his actions. He talked about his dedication to law and order, peace and security. The agency ate it up. They didn't get many ex-cops coming through their doors. Wannabe cops, sure. Skinny kids. Delusional paranoids. And weight-room types hyped up on steroids. Craig seemed the cream of the crop. They took him on straight away. Private security has been one of the few growth industries in Ottawa—or anywhere—recently. The agency needed a few half-decent men. Craig's been a Residential Security System Technician for over a year, meaning he drives around in a security cruiser in the wee hours, checking on the houses of Ottawa's well-to-do, making sure no one's messing with the elite's private property.

» » »

Back in the Hortons, the clerk recognizes Eddie. He blurts out right away, "Listen, man, I'm not interested. I'm flattered and all. A little bored most of the time, too. But it's just not my speed."

The kid's really earnest. Trying not to offend. He's had his sensitivity training. Eddie just stares at him, unstable on his feet. From the booze. From fatigue. From confusion.

"Two coffees. Black. Large." Eddie spills change from his pockets onto the counter.

The kid pours stale coffee into paper cups. Peers at Eddie.

"You okay, man? You don't look so good."

Eddie waves him away, pushes a couple two-dollar coins across the counter, leaves a bunch of pennies and silver lying there. He takes the coffees and heads back outside, sets the cups on the roof of his car, fumbles for his keys, then stops, leans left and vomits rye, Coke and Timbits all over the dirty grey snow. He pukes twice. Coughs. Passes barf through his nose. Spittle hangs from his lips. He wipes it away with the sleeve of his coat, and rights himself as best he can. The kid in the store looks out at him, shaking his head. Eddie grabs the coffees, ducks into the car and peels away towards Canadian Tire.

» » »

Inside the security cruiser, Eddie hands Craig the coffees. It's just after four in the morning. Craig takes the lids off both, opens the door and empties each cup halfway. He grabs a bottle of rye from under his seat and tops up the cups. Gives one to Eddie.

"Drink up, my man, then start yakking."

Eddie does as instructed, gulping the wretched brew. "I'll get right to the point. It's about my sister. I think I told you befores how she's sick. I'm all she's got right now. Cyril—the prick she married—is fucking around on her. I'm sure of it. Got no evidence but I don't need none. He leaves her almost every night to piss herself to sleep while he goes out and fucks whores. She calls me on the cell to come tend to her, fetch her shit. Like I'm her servant. It's eatin' me up inside."

Eddie pauses, takes another mouthful of rye and Timmys. Then starts again. "I want to fuck the guy up, Craig. My blood's boiling over this. Cyril deserves a shit kicking. Shelley'll never leave him but I want that fucker stopped. He can't do this to her. He needs a serious . . . what's the word for it?"

"Deterrent?"

"Yeah. Deterrent."

Craig, pauses, sips his drink and looks over at Eddie. "Why you want me involved?"

"Simple," Eddie goes. "If I laid the beating on him, Shelley'd never forgive me. She knows he's up to no good. Knows he deserves it. But it'd kill her if I did it. Push her right over the edge. She's weak enough as it is."

Craig nods. "What's in it for me? I don't want your money, you know that. You don't got the money to give me anyways."

Eddie nods. Knows it. Looks at his coffee cup. "Don't play smart," Eddie says. "I know how you like to get your kicks."

"When we gonna do this then?"

"Now," Eddie says. "Before I change my mind. Before I lose my nerve."

Eddie tries to look out the front window of the car but it's mostly fogged-up.

A few minutes later, Craig says, "So, Edward, where we gonna find this Cyril?"

They're still in the parking lot outside Canadian Tire.

"I figure he'll be down on Gladstone, scoping out the whores. Cyril's not too smart. Cheap, too. He's wouldn't use an agency. Probably takes them right off the street. The real dirties. And he works at Tunneys, so it's not too far."

"If he's still out, he shouldn't be hard to find. Hardly a soul stirring at this hour."

Eddie rubs his hands together. Wipes the sleeve of his coat across his lips. Thinks of his sister. Swallows. Turns to Craig. "Let's do it."

» » »

Craig's security cruiser in the dark could pass for a legit cop car, at least to the unwise, like Cyril. When they get down to Gladstone, there are only a few girls still out, sucking on butts, stamping their feet to stay warm, trying to make their quota before checking out for the night.

Craig and Eddie trawl the street looking for Cyril. Doesn't take them long. At Kent and Gladstone a car is pulled over, two wheels up on the curb, lights off, exhaust spewing from the tailpipe.

"That the perp?" Craig asks. "Should we move in on him? On your command, captain."

"Knock off the bullshit talk, Craig. Yeah, that's Cyril's car all right. The fucker. That's our man."

Craig barks, "Well, I've got my orders. Let me handle this. Here's how it's gonna play out. I'm gonna circle the block. Drop you off. Then go back and make like a real cop and intervene. This brother-in-law of yours really the shit-for-brains you say he is, he won't notice I'm not Ottawa Police. Chuck him in the back. Drive around a bit, have a few words. Put a scare into him, then dump him back at his car. Then come back and pick you up in ten minutes. Sound like a plan, ace?"

Eddie doesn't have much time to think. Plus he's still sozzled on all the rye. But he remembers his intent. "Sure,

Craig, drop me off. But remember: just fuck him up. Nothing too serious. Scare him shitless more than anything. A bit of a beating but don't break any fuckn bones. And tell him to stop his whoring around. Tell him he don't, it'll be worse next time. Just a deterrent. Pull your tough-guy routine."

Craig, driving along Florence Street, says, "Sure thing. I'll send him a message. You can count on it."

At Bank and Gladstone Eddie hops out.

Craig points. "Look, Eddie, a Hortons. Why don't you get us all some coffees while you're waiting?" He laughs.

Eddie's heartbeat quickens. "Don't get smart, Craig. Let's keep it simple. Do your work and then we'll call it a night."

Eddie slams the cruiser door, watches Craig drive away. The thought crosses his mind that Craig ignored every word he said.

» » »

Eddie and Shelley have always been close. Even though she's older, Eddie's always felt he had to look out for her just to make sure she never got hurt. Stems from their childhood. Once a drunk neighbour—the father of a friend of Shelley's—popped a gasket and jumped Shelley, wrestling her to the ground on the front lawn outside their house on Chatham Street in the west end of Hamilton.

When Eddie came bounding down the porch stairs, all of twelve years old, he thought the prick was trying to rape her. Then Eddie stopped and listened to the old coot.

"You stay aways from my daughter you lesbo whore. She said you taught her to do that to herself. That ain't right. Not decent behaviour. I oughta tan your hide seeing as your old lady won't do nothin' about it."

Eddie remembers it as clear as yesterday. He tackled the prick. Knocked him off Shelley and told her to run into the house and call their mom at work. The old guy did a somersault and then turned on Eddie. Male on male, he thought there was no reason to hold back. Hauled off and slugged Eddie in the mouth. Eddie spit blood but kept his fists up. Took two more shots before another neighbour stepped in. Eddie didn't say a word, had no idea what Shelley was up to with the neighbour's kid. Didn't really care. But didn't want her dirty laundry aired on the street, either. The drunk stumbled off home when the other neighbour mentioned calling the cops. The whole thing blew over quickly. It wasn't out of the ordinary for their street.

» » »

Eddie stands bleary-eyed at the corner of Bank and Gladstone. Slumped over, he looks like an insomniac rent boy. A minute later tires crunch, breaking his trance.

Craig's cruiser skids in the snow by the curb. He throws open the passenger door, glares at Eddie. "Get in! A slight change in plans. Bit of a problem."

Eddie can't speak. The anxiety, the stress, tightens his muscles, dries his throat. Craig reaches forward and grabs Eddie's jacket, hauling him inside the car. He slams the car into gear and they take off down Bank, make a right on Catherine and veer onto the highway, heading west. Cyril lies in a bloody heap in the backseat.

》 》 》

Off the highway, on Carling, Craig slows the security cruiser down to fifty klicks. He turns north on Churchill.

Eddie reaches over, clenching Craig's right forearm. "What the fuck happened? I thought I was pretty clear about what to do. He's not dead is he? Fuck sakes, Craig."

"Eddie, listen, it's not that bad. He's fine. He freaked is all when I pulled up. Started resisting when I tried to put him in the car. The whore scattered and ran. She knows better. But Cyril took a fuckn swing at me. I told you I don't go for that shit. I had to lay a beating on him just to subdue him, just to shut him up. Can you imagine what woulda happened if the real cops showed? So I clocked him a few times is all. Put the boots to him, too. Then tossed him in the back. He's unconscious. But you were bang on. Before the whore pissed off she spit something about him being one of her best customers. No, 'a regular' is how she put it. There's nothing *best* about that scumbag in the backseat my friend."

Eddie's head swims. He's lost control. Craig's calling the shots.

"What you got in mind, Craig?"

"Tell me where your sister lives. We go there. Sort it out. Make sure he's all right and then take him inside. I'll handle it. I'll make like a cop again. Your sister'll buy it. I'll tell her Cyril walked into a door or something."

"Fuck no, leave her out of it."

"Suit yourself."

Eddie considers his options for a second, then blurts, "No, you're right. We got no other choice. Let's dump him at their place. But you're sure he's not seriously hurt, eh?"

"Fuck, no. A couple bumps and bruises is all. He'll live."

» » »

Outside Shelley's place, Eddie and Craig sit watching the small townhouse, considering their exact plan of action— how Craig will get rid of Cyril without too much of a ruckus. Cyril is still comatose in the backseat.

"Could use a drink, Eddie," Craig says at last. It's nearly six o'clock in the morning. "Why don't you go get us a bottle from inside. Least we could do is drink the fucker's booze. That'll clear my head, get me thinking straight. Maybe you could check on your sister while you're at it."

Eddie stares at the house. He blows into his palms and then rubs his hands together. Starts thinking about Cyril and his whoring. About how the slut called him a regular. Thinks about Cyril sticking his cock in street scum while his wife—Eddie's sister—flounders in her own piss on the living room floor. Thinks about Shelley calling him at all hours to help her out. About all the times he's had to clean her up. Fetch her things. Give her meds. About all the nights when he could have been out trying to get laid. About his ex-wife and how she took off and left him high and dry. About Cheryl at work and her big, fat ass. About how he never got around to fucking her ass proper. About the sleazy cougars at Puzzles that he couldn't get it up for. About his mother. About the punk kid in Hortons. About the nagging, dark ache in his guts that just won't go away. No matter how much booze, no matter how many times he beats off—the ache in his gut just gets worse and worse. Eddie is—as junk psychologists say—*conflicted*. Maybe in need of a little closure.

"Be right back," Eddie says.

» » »

Over a bottle of peach schnapps, Eddie and Craig have a heart to heart like they used to back on the cleaning job.

"Tell me again about them snowmobilers," Eddie starts.

Craig smirks. "Fuck that shit. I'll tell you what you really want to know, big man. You wanna know what it's like to fuck someone against their will, right? That's what's running through that dirty little mind of yours, Eddie."

Eddie doesn't say anything. Doesn't meet Craig's eyes either. He looks, instead, at his sister's place.

"I'll come clean with you, Edward, dear—so to speak. It's the same reason I liked being a cop. The work was boring as fuck, especially out there in Hastings. But the power. You get to fuck up people's lives. The power, it goes to your head. It goes to your nuts. After a while the two meet and then there's no turning back. You really wanna know what it's like, Edward?" At this, Craig reaches over and puts two fingers under Eddie's chin, turning his head like a child's so they're face to face.

"It's fuckn sweet revenge my friend. And better with a man than a woman 'cause it fucks a man up way worse. I think you know what I mean. It's one fine piece of punishment, not to mention a great kick."

Eddie says nothing. He just keeps blowing on his hands and rubbing them together. He sucks on the bottle of schnapps as if it was his mother's tit.

Ten minutes later, the bottle of schnapps polished off, Craig quietly says, "Let's dump him and me and you go out and party proper. I know a place down on Lisgar where I can introduce you to some friends of mine. Get you what you need. Even at this hour."

Eddie, mad-drunk—buzzing wildly on booze, caffeine, sugar and sleep deprivation—turns to Craig, "Not now. Let's just get rid of Cyril."

"You sure about that?"

"For the moment. I want this over with."

"Right. Help me get him to the front door of your sister's and then go back and duck down in the car while I handle it from there."

» » »

In the dim light of pre-dawn—not a paperboy, not a snowplough, not a dog-walker in sight—Eddie and Craig stagger as they drag Cyril's limp body up the walkway toward the townhouse. Halfway there, Cyril comes to. He grunts and spits. Turns his bloodied face and stares at Eddie. Without missing a beat he blurts, "Knew you were behind this Eddie. Shitty stunt like this has your fingerprints all over it. Break Shelley's heart when she hears it."

Cyril, bloodied and beaten, still has the balls to play his trump. Eddie peers at him through eyes reduced to slits. Again images flood his brain: Shelley covered in piss; their dead mother barking orders at him; the neighbour from way back calling Shelley a lesbo.

Staring at Cyril, Eddie says, "Take him round back to the tool shed, Craig. Let's finish the fucker off right."

Craig nods. "Music to my ears, Edward my dear."

» » »

Cyril is gagged with oily lawnmower rags, bound at the wrists with an extension cord and facedown on the stone-cold, mid-winter concrete floor of the tool shed. Eddie says, "Show me how you did it with them snowmobilers, Craig." It comes out flat, dead calm—barely anything lustful or vengeful about it.

Craig drops to his knees, hauls Cyril's pants down, exposing his white ass. Cyril moans in protest, writhes like a stuck fish in the bottom of a boat.

"You gotta hold him a bit for me," Craig says. "That's how we always did it. At least when they were conscious. Took turns. One guy sits on him while the other has a go."

Eddie says, "Can't do it that way. I wanna watch . . . Learn." He grabs hedge clippers and stuffs them into Cyril's crotch. "Move an inch Cyril and I'll cut your cock off and stick it in your ear."

Craig regards him. "You sick fuck."

Eddie looks down at Craig's pants. "Don't look like it bothers you none."

Cyril's barely breathing. Not moving a muscle.

"This's how we did it out Marmora way," Craig

growls, lunging forward, elbow-smashing Cyril to the back of the head. Cyril's teeth smash against the concrete. He groans and slips back into unconsciousness.

Craig pulls down his pants and his cock springs out, hard and fierce. Eddie looks at it, drops to his knees and puts it in his mouth, slobbering all over it, lubing Craig up. Then Eddie turns and vomits, barfing on the concrete right by Cyril's head. Eddie falls to his knees, then all the way down to his belly. Face mashed into his own puke. Turns and looks over at Cyril and Craig. Sees the strain on Craig's face as the big man pushes his cock into the crack of Cyril's ass. Cyril spasms for a moment, then lies still. Eddie tries to speak but his mouth is gooey and he can't speak, cannot move. He watches, eyes watering, nose clogged, as Craig pounds away at Cyril's downed body. It hardly lasts a minute before Craig's done. He rolls off Cyril, collapses. Then grins at Eddie.

"You ready, big fella?"

Eddie looks at Craig. He spits out bits of barf and phlegm to clear his mouth. Thinks of his sister. Of bittersweet, confused revenge.

Craig smiles. "Your turn, then, Edward my dear."

Eddie swallows hard—bile rising to his mouth. Then forces himself to his hands and knees.

» » »